Control

Also from K. Bromberg

Control

An Everyday Heroes Novella

By K. Bromberg

1001 Dark Nights

EVIL EYE
CONCEPTS

Control: An Everyday Heroes Novella
By K. Bromberg

1001 Dark Nights

Copyright 2018 JKB Publishing, LLC
ISBN: 978-1-948050-39-5

Foreword: Copyright 2014 M. J. Rose

Published by Evil Eye Concepts, Incorporated

Sign up for the 1001 Dark Nights Newsletter
and be entered to win a Tiffany Key necklace.

There's a contest every month!

Go to www.1001DarkNights.com to subscribe.

As a bonus, all subscribers will receive a free copy of
Discovery Bundle Three
Featuring stories by
Sidney Bristol, Darcy Burke, T. Gephart
Stacey Kennedy, Adriana Locke
JB Salsbury, and Erika Wilde

One Thousand and One Dark Nights

Once upon a time, in the future…

*I was a student fascinated with stories and learning.
I studied philosophy, poetry, history, the occult, and
the art and science of love and magic. I had a vast
library at my father's home and collected thousands
of volumes of fantastic tales.*

*I learned all about ancient races and bygone
times. About myths and legends and dreams of all
people through the millennium. And the more I read
the stronger my imagination grew until I discovered
that I was able to travel into the stories… to actually
become part of them.*

*I wish I could say that I listened to my teacher
and respected my gift, as I ought to have. If I had, I
would not be telling you this tale now.
But I was foolhardy and confused, showing off
with bravery.*

*One afternoon, curious about the myth of the
Arabian Nights, I traveled back to ancient Persia to
see for myself if it was true that every day Shahryar
(Persian: شهريار, "king") married a new virgin, and then
sent yesterday's wife to be beheaded. It was written
and I had read, that by the time he met Scheherazade,
the vizier's daughter, he'd killed one thousand
women.*

Something went wrong with my efforts. I arrived in the midst of the story and somehow exchanged places with Scheherazade — a phenomena that had never occurred before and that still to this day, I cannot explain.

Now I am trapped in that ancient past. I have taken on Scheherazade's life and the only way I can protect myself and stay alive is to do what she did to protect herself and stay alive.

Every night the King calls for me and listens as I spin tales. And when the evening ends and dawn breaks, I stop at a point that leaves him breathless and yearning for more. And so the King spares my life for one more day, so that he might hear the rest of my dark tale.

As soon as I finish a story... I begin a new one... like the one that you, dear reader, have before you now.

Prologue

Reznor

"It wasn't your fault, Rez."

"Easy for you to say." I look over to my supervisor, Harry, and take in the pained look on his face, but I don't really care. "I made the call to breach. Their blood is on my hands."

"That's bullshit, and you know it." Laughter in the bullpen outside his office filters in, so he walks the few steps and shuts the door hard enough for the cheap metal mini blinds to make a noise as they bounce back against its glass. "It was the fucker who did this's fault."

"Mm-hmm." I keep my eyes on my hands, but with her scream so loud in my head it could be blood on my cuticles and not the grease from working on my motorcycle earlier that I stare at. "I need some time off. A month or two. I don't know."

His chuckle is dismissive. "Guys like you don't take time off, Reznor. You're a throwback. You've been doing this, what? Twelve years?"

"Fifteen."

"Fifteen. How many times in my tenure here have I heard you say you want time off only to come back the next day?"

"It doesn't matter. What matters is I'm asking now." I roll my shoulders because I was right. He was going to fight me on this.

"You're the team leader. You just can't—"

"Paul will do just fine stepping into my shoes for a bit."

"He's not you though. In case you haven't noticed, it seems like we're in a wave of serious shit right now. One fucking thing after another. The calls aren't stopping…Christ." He puts his hands on his hips and stares at the guys in the pen. They're ribbing each other and laughing when fuck if

I know how long it's been since I've gotten a solid night's sleep. "They depend on you."

I nod, the guilt already eating at me that I'm going to let my men down. "I know."

His sigh is heavy and weighs down the room. "I can't do it right now. I can't let you step away so you keep reliving everything that went down. You're going to get in your own head over it, and that's gonna fuck you up further. You'll walk away."

"I won't walk away." The thought has crossed my mind more times than not these past few sleepless weeks.

"We have shrinks here you can talk to. Department ones who know the stress you're going through."

"I've been there, done that."

"Not with this case you haven't. C'mon. I'll make you an appointment." He moves to the phone and picks it up as if he's calling.

"Shrinks who will take everything I say and use it against me to put me in some desk in the gun locker or file archives."

"I wouldn't allow that."

"Doesn't mean it wouldn't happen."

"Rez—"

"If you don't give me time off, then I quit."

The speed at which his head whips up tells me he heard me loud and clear this time. "What do you mean, *you quit*? That's fucking hilarious."

I shove up from my seat, and that sudden wave of panic, which feels like a constant part of me these days, rises up and threatens to take over. His smile fades and his eyebrows narrow when he sees I'm dead serious.

"Rez, what's going on?"

I shove a hand through my hair and shake my head. "I don't know."

But I do know. It's the constant doubt that I messed up and my fuck-up took someone else's life.

Children's lives. Innocent kids who had a lifetime of possibilities stretched before them.

"I've never seen you step away. You're always taking extra shifts. You're always here even when you're off training the newbies. This is your place."

"That's the saddest statement I've ever heard." I chuckle, but it just sounds desperate...when I'm not a desperate man. "Maybe I do need to quit, so I can get some kind of life other than wanting to hang out with this bunch of assholes." I look out the window at my crew. I know them better than some of their wives do. I trust my life with them and to them.

But fuck if that drive within me isn't gone, and I have no clue how to find it again. And for a long time, that was all I needed. *All that motivated me.*

"Don't quit, Rez," he says. He holds up his hand for me to wait, while he sits behind his massive desk that looks impressive but would probably fall apart with one solid slam of the drawers.

"Why? People get killed on my watch, Sarge."

"You've had a bad string of crazies. They aren't your fault."

"No, but not saving lives is."

"Are you doubting yourself?" His eyes bore into mine and make me want to look away, but hell if his words aren't the truth right now.

Hell yes, I doubt myself. And why the fuck wouldn't I?

"Just give me some time."

Harry doesn't relent, because he knows what's going on. He knows the more time I take away, the more likely I won't be able to find my way back.

He shuffles some papers, and when he finds the one he's searching for, he takes a minute to read it through. He twists his lips as if he's trying to figure something out for a moment before lifting his eyes to meet mine. "I have an offer for you."

"I won't take it."

A raise won't fix this.

"Just hear me out." He holds up his hands in front of him, telling me to be patient. When I don't move from the chair, he continues. "It's a change of pace. A change in scenery. It's all right here…"

Chapter One

Desi

Men are on women.

Women are on women.

Grunts and groans fill the air.

There is cheering from the sidelines as bystanders watch them writhe and buck and try to get the other off them.

"It's like a big orgy in here," I say to the woman standing beside me. I don't know her, but she's standing like we are, back against the gym wall, eyes glued to the men and women fighting for positioning—moving, bucking, defending—on the mats where they're lying.

She emits a nervous laugh and looks to me. Prim and proper, she resembles a Stepford wife, and all I can think is that her ladies' club decided to do this together and she's the only one who decided to show up.

At least I'm not the only one nervous about being here. There could be worse things I guess…like actually needing to use the skills I'm supposed to learn here in Sunnyville Self Defense Class to protect myself.

A group at the far side of the gym erupts in applause, and I stand on my tiptoes to see a woman standing with her foot on the instructor's throat while he's lying on the mat. His red SSDC T-shirt matches everyone else standing around trying to look official with a whistle and gym pants on.

"Exactly," a deep rumble of a voice on the other side of me says.

I glance over and *whoa*…all my attention shifts from the grunts and groans on the floor to how I wouldn't mind grunting and groaning with the man on his cell beside me. Our gazes meet for the briefest of seconds—chocolate-brown eyes giving me a passing glance and a curt smile before turning back to whoever is on the phone while watching the action beyond.

Taking my time and trying not to pay attention to Hottie McTotty, I scan the gym. Basic blue gymnastic mats cover the majority of the hardwood floors, basketball hoops hang from the lofty ceiling but have been drawn up, and championship banners hang, partially hiding the painted mural of the Sunnyville High School mascot on the wall at the far end.

But no matter how hard I try to not look back at him, that is where my attention lands. He's a good six inches taller than I am, has dark hair, and his body beneath his Under Armour workout shirt hints at how ridiculously fit he is. His bicep closest to me stretches the fabric and is covered in a dizzying tattooed array of colors and images I can't openly look at to decipher. *You can only do so much with a sideways stare.*

But his voice. It's like liquid sex with a rasp and a rumble and a whole earth-shattering orgasm in between.

Hello to you, Mister A-Little-Rugged-And-Whole-Lot-Sexy.

I listen to him talk. Not stalkerish-like...well, maybe stalkerish-like, but damn if the background of grunting and groaning only serves to enhance the things my mind is dreaming up.

And then it hits me.

He's not here as an instructor—no red SSDC shirt on. So that means he's here as a boyfriend or a husband and therefore completely off limits.

Damn it.

If he were an instructor, I'd make sure to be in his group so he could grind on me for a bit...and I'm talking the pelvis kind of grind...if I'm being truthful.

He ends his call, and when he goes to put his cell in his pocket, he catches me staring at him, because I'm still stuck on the fact that he's waiting for his girl.

"Hello."

God, that voice.

"Hi." I smile brightly, and I'm sure when I straighten up my tits arch out in reflex.

He notices. I know he does, but what do I care? It's not like I have a chance with him.

"Are you taking a class?" he asks.

"I'm supposed to." I shrug and shift on my feet, suddenly nervous when I have no reason to be. "But I'm not sure how much I'll learn."

"No?" He turns to look at me, eyebrows raised, lips pursed.

"It's Sunnyville." His eyes are unrelenting as they bore into mine. "It's not like we attract the best talent." He angles his head to the side, mouth ghosting a smile I can't read, as if he's questioning if he made the right investment by putting his loved one here. "That's not what I mean."

"Then what do you mean?" He turns to face me, clasped hands hanging in front of his pelvis, and my eyes flicker there for the briefest of moments.

To his hands. To avert my gaze from the intensity in his. Not to blatantly stare at his cock…but of course when I look back up to his eyes and see the lift of his brow and a smile toying at the corners of his mouth, he assumes I was checking out his package.

Lovely.

"I mean"—I look at the crowded gym while my nerves rattle harder. When my nerves rattle my mouth runs, and when my mouth runs, I can't be held accountable for what I say. "These instructors are all wanna-be cops. They probably never passed the exam to get into the Academy." His smile grows wider and my lady bits might be tingling as I peg this guy to be one who likes to live a little dangerously. Maybe he's had a run-in or two with the law and places cops not high on his list of people to invite to dinner.

"Rent-a-cops?" he asks through a part-cough, part chuckle.

"Yeah, those. Either that or they're the guys who couldn't pass the psych test and are a little wacky."

He purses his lips as if he's measuring my words and when he shakes his head with a laugh, that grin of his widens to epic proportions. "Definitely the psych test."

"Right? I mean, I get they're here trying to help women protect themselves, but you'd think they might have a tiny part of them who gets off on the power play aspect of it." *Stop talking, Desi. Your best friend-in-law is a police officer. You know differently.* And yet my mouth still runs because he's cute. "You know…pushing women around. Taking their abuse. It's probably a turn-on for some of them."

He nods slowly and surveys the room with a lift of his eyebrows. "That's what you seriously think?"

A round of applause erupts and echoes throughout the entire room before I get a chance to answer him. I'm forced to step backward when the slew of women who just finished with their session heads to where we are standing near the door.

When the influx of chatty women seemingly excited and high on adrenaline—despite their sweat-dampened hair and flushed cheeks—finally clears the doorway he's nowhere to be found.

It's a blanket reminder that he definitely was here to pick up his significant other. Add to that, I just acted like a complete idiot trying to impress a man who I'll undoubtedly see around town again and cringe when I do.

Since when do I try to impress people?

"The seven o'clock group can head on in," a man says as he motions to all of us standing against the wall.

All it takes are those words to make my mind shift gears—because if I'm one thing, it's hard on myself before I move on to the next thing—and coming here is a major step in admitting that what happened scared the shit out of me.

With a roll of my shoulders and a huff of a breath, I step forward with the women beside me. We find seats on the mat as directed and wait for everyone to settle.

The gentleman who summoned us stands with his hands on his hips. His bald head is shinier than Mr. Clean's, and he has tree trunks for arms. With a clap of his hands in front of him, he begins. "Congratulations, ladies, on taking the first step in taking back your fear. People call me Bear. Yes, it's odd, but just go with it." He smiles wide and takes a step forward as three men in SSDC shirts file in behind him. "Some of you are here because you've had a scare and need a way to erase that helplessness you were made to feel. Others are here because you saw a movie, a news story—something that made you not want to ever be in the position to be made a victim. So let's get one thing straight: no one here is a victim. Every single one of you here is strong. And we're here to show you just how strong you are."

I glance at the women and wonder who fits what profile. Who's been victimized? Women from all walks of life and sizes and ethnicities surround me—some I know, most I don't—and it calms me some knowing I'm not alone in this. That I'm not ridiculous in being scared.

"Let me introduce to you our four instructors so you know who you'll be giving hell today." A round of chuckles filters through the air. "First up I have Teddy. He's a Krav Maga instructor by day and a self-defense teacher at night. He's been doing this for fifteen years and loves nothing more than for you to beat up on him." Teddy, with the light hair and slender build, lifts his hand in greeting.

"Hello, Teddy," a woman near me says with a whistle and fans her hand in front of her face.

"He's happily married, as well."

"Damn," she murmurs and gets a round of chuckles, nerves tingeing the edges of most of them.

"Next up is Eric. He's a newly minted instructor, and so I told him you'd be easy on him," Bear says, all the while shaking his head to tell us not to. "He might be new, but the kid somehow has endless requests from women to be placed with him."

Eric steps forward and lifts his hand. He's tall with the looks of a model—chiseled, scruff, blinding smile—but too clean-cut for my liking. "That's only because I give out free candy at the end of class," he says, as the women sit taller and pat down their hair.

I'm sure his lollipop is what he has to offer.

And then I feel stupid even thinking that. It's my damn nerves again. They're making me jittery and causing my thoughts to run. The last thing any of these women are here for is to be enjoying the eye-candy.

They're here to learn self-defense.

They're here to prepare themselves.

Then why am I looking?

Because you're really good at sticking your head in the sand and using other things to distract you from the truth.

The truth that says you're scared but too stubborn to admit it.

"Next up is Ky. He's straight from Florida where he's a physical therapist for the Olympic athletes, and now he's doubling as an instructor for the next few months."

Ky lifts his arm. His light brown skin is gorgeous in color, and his arms are dotted with Maori tattoos.

"And last but not least is our newest addition. A certified badass who has served as the commander of one of San Francisco's SWAT units for fifteen years before recently taking a short sabbatical to live a life outside of the constant razor's edge of crazies. We're thrilled to have him and his expertise. Ladies, please welcome Reznor."

The ladies clap, and I turn to find none other than the tattooed hottie who was standing by the door with me. *Oh shit.* Now with the red company shirt on, he takes his time walking over to us while every part of me wants to crawl in a hole and die of embarrassment.

My comments loop on a reel in my head as I lower my eyes and shut them momentarily.

Did I really say all that about cops and psych tests and…oh, this is not good.

And of course when I lift my eyes again, he is staring right at me. No mistaking it. He doesn't address us, but rather just holds my gaze, and with a ghost of that smile of his, nods his head before stepping back.

Reznor.

How did I know he'd have a sexy name to go with all that deliciousness that he is?

The ladies turn their focus back to Bear and just before I do, Reznor gives the subtlest lift of his eyebrows to me as if to challenge what I'd said before turning his attention to his job.

Bastard.

Chapter Two

Desi

Of course I was placed in his group.

Placed in his group and too damn proud to ask that I be changed to a different instructor.

Isn't that karma for you? To be put in the group with the man I probably insulted seven ways from Sunday? It's not like I can fake interaction with him. It's not like I can be a wallflower against the mascot mural and blend in until I disappear.

The man is going to have his hands on me. He's going to be physical with me.

And hell if I didn't make a bed I'm going to have to lie in.

Shit.

For some reason I don't think sticking my head in the sand is going to get me out of this situation.

A blue mat on a gym floor isn't exactly the horizontal action I had in my brief although extensive fantasy of him.

"So, as Bear said, I'm a SWAT team commander. I like long walks off short piers, chasing parked cars, oh, and babies and puppies are my kryptonite." He chuckles with the rest of the women, who are shifting on their feet as he tries to put them at ease. "But seriously, I've spent my career trying to save people from or trying to get people out of harm's way. In all this time, there's one thing I've learned: *it can happen to anyone.* There is no profile for who will be mugged. No stereotype for who will be raped. No anything to pinpoint who will be next." He pauses and lets the weight of his words sink in before he claps his hands together loud enough to make us jump.

Shrieks of surprise turn to nervous laughter. The lady next to me startles, and her hand flies to her throat, an "Oh, dear" falling from her mouth. I reach over to pat her back comfortingly, all while my eyes stay right on Reznor as he walks from one end of the mat to the other.

"And that's why I want to congratulate you on being here. On taking that first step of being in control of you." As he speaks he meets the eyes of every woman in the line, and when he gets to where I am standing on the end, gives a subtle shake of his head, but his eyes give away nothing of the words I said to him earlier. "Over the next few weeks, we'll be learning several different aspects of self-defense. You won't learn everything overnight, and that's okay. We'll take our time so that you'll feel confident in knowing what to do in case you need to use it. If at any point you're unsure, please don't hesitate to ask. Right, so let's get started."

He begins with some basic information—how to hold your fist when you punch, the most sensitive parts on a male body to hit, etcetera—and then asks us to remove our shoes so we can begin.

"Okay, I need a volunteer to help with the demonstration."

Hands shoot up all around me. Smart women. Who wouldn't want his undivided attention? I'd normally be elbowing through the women with both arms raised to make sure I'm seen and maybe give a crass one-liner to guarantee my selection.

But that was before I made an ass of myself with him. I refuse to lower my head and hide, but hell if I'm going to be his "body" to demonstrate with.

And just as the thought crosses my mind, Reznor, with his bright eyes and sarcasm-laced smile, steps directly into my field of vision.

"Thank you for volunteering," he says, and I shake my head in protest.

"No, I'm fine. I'll watch."

Did I really say he probably failed his psych evaluation?

The smile that's toying on his lips tells me yes. Yes, I did.

Crap.

"I don't take no for an answer when it comes to making sure you're prepared." This time he puts on the brightest smile so everyone sees the charming man trying to get me to participate, while I see the gleam in his eye that says he can't wait to challenge me and prove me wrong.

He reaches his hand out to me and rather than take it, out of principle, I look at it and then step past him onto the mat and face the ladies standing there with envious eyes.

Reznor moves toward me. "What's your name?"

"Desi," I say begrudgingly, wondering why I feel so hostile toward him when I was the ass in our conversation.

"Desi. Nice to meet you." He holds out his hand for me to shake, and I know more than anything he is seeing if I'll acquiesce in this silent battle of wills we have going on.

And of course I do. I tell myself it's only because people are watching, but I grab his hand, squeeze strongly, and shake, all the while trying to ignore the warmth of his skin and the size of his hands.

"Now, let's imagine that Desi here is walking through a parking garage late one night," he says as he walks from one side of the mat, passes behind me, and then to the other side. "She's busy checking her text messages on her cell and not paying attention to her surroundings. And out of the blue—"

Suddenly his hand is over my mouth, and his other arm has grabbed my midsection and yanked me back against him. I yelp. Fuck.

No.

He's too close.

I know where I am. I know who he is. But regardless, panic flickers through me. The kind that makes your mind blank and your heart lurch into your throat.

The kind I felt when I woke up to find the dark shadow standing at the foot of my bed a few weeks ago.

"Deep breath," Reznor murmurs in my ear when he feels my body tense and hears my startled gasp. "I'm not going to hurt you."

It's stupid, but his simple words put me at ease, and I hate that I need to be given that feeling.

"Desi is now in a parking garage without a soul in sight and a man who is going to what? I don't know what each of you has been through, why you're here, so I'm not going to spell out potential scenarios. But right now, she's going to become a victim." My heart thunders in my throat as his arms tense around me. "Show me what you would do."

For a woman who typically loves being the center of attention, I absolutely hate the feeling of it right now. Everyone's eyes are on me, and all I can think is how the last thing I want is to do the wrong thing and show them how in fact I would be dead.

Stupid? *Yes.* The truth? *Definitely.*

"Desi?" he murmurs and for the life of me, I don't know why I do it—why instead of stomping on his instep or throwing my elbow backward, or even trying to twist miraculously away from him so I can knee him in the nuts—I force my tongue out of my covered mouth and lick the palm of his hand.

I feel him startle, and he loosens his grip in surprise. Just when I begin to wiggle out of his grasp, he's on me again, but this time, I end up on my back on the mat with a *thud*. He looms over me with a disbelieving look on his face while I catch the breath that has just *whooshed* out of me with his move.

Yep. He's still handsome.

And I'm now flat on my ass looking up at him.

"You see," Reznor says to our group as he offers me a hand to pull me up, "Desi tried to get cute. And the shock value might work in some instances. She licked my palm, and it sure as hell caught me off guard, but it wasn't the safest action to take. If I'm a sexual predator high on adrenaline, it might turn me on even further."

I take a little bow, owning the criticism because hell if hearing him say I might turn him on isn't something that's on repeat in my head. I'll use any distraction I can get to take my mind off the fear just being put in that position evoked in me.

"You can curtsy all you want," Reznor says with a sarcastic tone and a shake of his head, "but it's not going to save your ass."

My spine stiffens at his comment. "Loosen up, I was joking." I roll my eyes for added humor but when I look back to him, there is absolutely no amusement in his expression.

"I'd love to *loosen up*"—he turns to face me—"but that would mean you wouldn't be getting what you came here for. To learn how to fight back and defend yourself. The comedy club is that way if you want to be the funny girl and make jokes." He hooks a thumb over his shoulder as the two of us wage a visual war. "Because roughly seven out of ten women will be assaulted in their lifetime…of the ten of you standing here, seven have already or at some point will be a victim… Now, I might not be a genius, but I put my money on the fact that they want to be taught what to do." He pauses as my eyes burn into his. "Shall we continue?"

No one likes to feel stupid.

And of course that's how I feel, but hell if I'll give him the satisfaction of knowing how hard I want to pull that stick out of his ass when he's right on the money.

"Then maybe you should tell me what to do." I sound snotty when I speak no matter how hard I try. Because there's being chastised, and then there's being chastised by the man you were pseudo hitting on earlier. Now, no matter how hard you tell yourself it isn't the case, you feel a little rejected.

He flashes me a brilliant smile that grates on my nerves. "Gladly."

And for the next hour and odd minutes, I'm on my back. Up against a wall. Up against him. Any way you can imagine it, Reznor uses me as his dummy to demonstrate what to do, and what not to do.

All with his body against mine.

"That's all for today's class. Ladies, I hope you learned something today, but remember your number one goal is to escape to safety, not fight. If your attacker is coming toward you, the three simplest moves you can use to defend yourself are the down slap to the forehead, the Dracula, and the throat strike. Stay safe and we'll see you next time."

A round of clapping starts, and all I do is sag in relief because I'm exhausted.

And pissed off.

I don't clap. I don't even look his way as I stalk off the mat and head toward the bleacher at the far end of the gym where my stuff is. Noise erupts as the other classes end and women begin chatting.

I need to get the hell out of here.

I'm tired. I'm sore. And…and I'm not sure how I feel, but I don't like it.

"Desi."

When he calls my name, I'm primed for a fight…especially with him.

"Go away," I mutter as I keep my head down, knowing how anything I do can and will be used against me. Sunnyville might not be a Podunk town, but it has one whopper of a gossip mill, and I'm the last person who wants to take center stage in it.

I take my time gathering my keys and water but can feel his presence at my back.

"Thanks for helping today."

I whip around to see him standing there, shirt off and balled in his hands, pants slung low on his hips, a towel scrubbing through his hair. The typical look of a guy who knows he has a hot body and is so damn comfortable with it he doesn't give a second thought that most people can't do that *and* look sexy.

"Helping?" I grit out. "How about being your human punching bag for the past hour? The one you continually said was doing the wrong thing. How about that, huh?"

He chuckles. "You're right. I'm sorry. I should have taught you nothing while I went and took my psych test again to see if I qualify for the Academy."

"You're an asshole."

"Same could be said about someone who judges others without giving them the benefit of the doubt," he says and shrugs nonchalantly.

"Look. I was making conversation. I was..." I run a hand through my hair and sigh as I rein in my temper. "Never mind."

Stop babbling, Des. That's what got you into this predicament in the first place.

"You better hope you never need to defend yourself—"

"Screw you."

"—because you're spending so much time being mad at me that you're not paying attention."

"I don't put myself in situations to..."

Reznor angles his head to the side and takes a step closer. "Ah, but you have though." His voice is softer, sympathetic. I take a step back and shake my head. "What did he do to you, Desi?"

"Who said anyone did anything to me?" I shove my hands on my hips to match my defensive tone.

He rocks on his heels and stares at me with an intensity I want to shy away from but don't dare. "You didn't have to say a word. It's written in your defiance...in your body language."

"Maybe my body language is saying I've had enough of you and your bullshit."

"Dodge and defend." He chuckles, and it grates on my nerves. "I should have figured you'd be one of *those*."

"One of *those*?"

"The person who can't admit you've been caught off guard. That you were vulnerable and someone else took advantage of it."

"I'm fine."

"Uh-huh. Types like you always quit," he says, prompting me to shove my keys in my purse and try to walk past him. But he sidesteps to block my exit. "All talk and no guts."

"I said it before, and I'll say it again...*screw you and your stereotypes.*"

"I'll be surprised if I see you again on Thursday."

I glare at him before stomping away. My resolve that I wasn't coming back is now shattered by my pure stubbornness to prove him wrong. *Arrogant asshole.*

The night air feels like heaven. It's still hot and stifling but it doesn't smell like sweaty gym, and it sure as hell doesn't smell like Reznor—cool and clean and manly.

Standing in the entry of the high school, all I can do is shake my head and curse the man I've tried to abuse over the last hour.

He frustrated me. He tested me. I tried to fight back.

I lost.

Is that why I'm pissed? Because he proved to me there's no way I could handle myself if I were attacked?

Or is it because he stood there, confronting and frustrating me, making me so angry I totally missed the opportunity to admire how freaking hot he is with his shirt off?

Because what I remember of him...*damn.*

Get a grip.

He's nothing.

You're fine and can handle yourself.

But when I start the car, there's a niggling feeling deep down that I know all of those are lies.

All three of them.

Chapter Three

Reznor

The beer is cold, the bar is crowded, and the music is some twangy shit that makes me feel like I'm back in the South…when I left its humid heat and sweet-talking women years ago.

Sweet talking. That sure as hell isn't what comes to mind when I think of Desi from last night…and yet, she's been on my mind more than I care to think about.

I nod subtly at the woman eyeing me and then shift to survey the local cop hangout, Hooligan's. There are definitely boys in blue in here—you can tell by their walk, their attitude, their need to blow off steam—and it feels so odd to be on the outside of the unspoken bond between the men when I'm usually right in the fucking middle. The nucleus. The one they come to when they need advice, to talk, anything…

But this isn't San Francisco.

This is Sunnyville, California. Home of grapes on the hills, wine in the cellars, and my temporary home for the next few months.

"Reznor fucking Mayne, is that you?"

Talk about a small world.

I turn to see an old friend from the Academy moving across the space. He's a little over six foot. Dark hair. Light eyes. The fucker has filled out since being in the same graduating class with me—when he knew this was what he was made to do, and I questioned whether I'd be able to stay on the right side of the law.

"Grant Malone? No shit."

We shake hands, and he takes a seat beside me. The bartender slides a beer to him within seconds without him asking.

"Thanks, Timmy," he says with a nod and then turns back to me. "You look good. What happened, did you have a run-in at a tattoo parlor?" He laughs as he takes in the sleeve covering my right arm.

"You know how it goes. We all have to tell our stories somewhere...mine just happens to be on my arms. Hell, if I've gotta be straight-laced, I might as well look like a badass while doing it."

"You haven't changed one bit." Grant lifts his beer to his lips and shakes his head.

"And your skin is still art free," I tease. "Still a cop?"

"Detective."

"No shit?"

"No shit."

"You like it?"

"It's a smaller beat but—"

"Crime's everywhere."

"You can say that again. I'm just coming off a homicide at one of the vineyards. Decided I'd kick it here for a bit, unwind, get my head straight before heading home to the fam."

"Family?" I'm not surprised. Malone's one of the good ones.

"Yep. Wife. Two kids with one on the way. Dogs."

"So very TV sitcom-ish."

We both laugh, the leap in our lives so very different than the last time we saw each other.

"What about you? You married? Kids?"

"Nah. Not sure if it's for me or not."

"I can respect that. Are you still on the right side of the law or did you decide it wasn't exciting enough for you?" he asks without any judgment in his tone. It doesn't surprise me that he remembers our late-night conversations in the Academy dorms. The ones where I confessed to what a punk I'd been. The trouble I'd been caught up in where I figured my only option was to sign on with the force or end up behind bars.

"Me? SWAT." I love the look on his face. Shock mixed with disbelief. "Wild, huh?"

"You're serious."

"As a heart attack. Did entry for ten years, and I've been the commander of a team with SFPD for the past five."

He looks at the beer between his hands and smiles. "Some of the guys took bets after we graduated from the Academy whether you'd stick it out or not."

"Nice to know my friends are bastard assholes," I say through a laugh, but know damn well I would have bet against me too. "And?"

"Looks like if I could track down the old crew, I'd be a rich man." He taps the neck of his beer against mine and takes a long pull before looking back at me. "Fucking SWAT, Rez? Really?"

"Yep. Gotta get my fix of adrenaline somehow." I take my time looking around the bar, watching to see who's sitting back, taking note of who's paying attention that Grant is talking to an outsider in this town where it seems everyone knows everyone. Getting the lay of the land even when I'm not on duty. It seems old habits die hard. "So this is your beloved Sunnyville, huh?"

"Yep. Big but small. Scenic but confining. A place where everyone knows your name...and your business." He laughs, but I can tell he loves it here. "Told you that you'd make it here one day."

"Guess it seems you knew all the answers back then. You should have been a fortune teller."

"No, thanks. I'm good with where life has brought me. What brings you here?"

"I took some time off I had coming."

"There's never time off in our world," he says, and I can see his mind working. I know he's wondering if I was put on disciplinary leave for something. It's really none of his fucking business, but the last thing I need is him looking into me.

"Shit went south in a situation I was leading my team on. A dad barricaded with kids. I made the call to breach. Shit went bad before we were able to neutralize him."

That much is the truth.

"It's not your fault."

Malone gets it. What's in my head. What keeps me up at night. Why I needed to leave the city behind for a little bit.

"Yeah. I know. It doesn't make it feel any better." I finish off my beer and shrug away the screaming echoing in my head from their mother as she stood behind the barricades fighting officers to get to her babies. "Just a fucking waste."

"It always is." He judges my mood with a nod and a tight smile. "I'm sorry."

"No need to be."

"So you took time off to get your head straight?"

"Something like that." I chuckle and then sigh, because I know I need to give more. "It was either that or I was going to quit so...it was agreed I'd take some time. Besides, my sergeant knew the head of a self-defense academy out here. He needed some instructors and my boss wanted to make sure I didn't fall off the damn grid. Figured, why not get the hell out of Dodge for a while and do that."

"Timing is everything."

"It most definitely is," I say as Grant points to my beer asking if I want another. I nod.

"Sunnyville Self Defense Class?"

"That would be the one."

"Bear's a good guy."

"You know him?" Small town. Everyone knows everyone.

"Yep. Does that mean you're going to be hanging around Sunnyville for a bit?"

"Seems like it. He has two instructors out on vacation, so I said I'd fill in."

"It's not like you don't know how to defend yourself."

"Are you still sore about that, Malone?" I tease, remembering our hand-to-hand combat lessons and how I beat him in the class competition.

"Nah." He smiles. "Grudges aren't my thing. You'll have to come over sometime. We can catch up, shoot the shit, talk about the old days..."

"You mean talk about kicking each other's asses."

"We had some good times."

"Fucking epic." I take a tug on my beer.

"It's a plan then. But for now, I've got to head home." He stands from his stool and sets a business card on the bar top before cuffing me on the shoulder. "Good seeing you again, Rez."

I pick up his card and turn it over in my hand as he walks away.

Sunnyville Police Department. Detective Grant Malone.

He's where he should be. Detective. Husband. Father. He's...Christ, he's happy. Fulfilled. Doing what he loves.

I shake my head and look around. *And what does that make you, Rez?* Hell if I know.

At one point my job was all I needed. But is that still all I need, or am I craving something more? Something else to give me that rush?

Fuck this.

Now's not time for psychological bullshit.

Now's time for another beer.

Chapter Four

Desi

"Des?"

I jump at the sound of my name and rap my head against the cabinet as the dogs lying in various places of the room jump and begin baying.

"Goddammit, Jeff. You scared the shit out of me." I stand with a hand pressed to the back of my hair and my heart pounding a violent staccato in my chest.

Thoughts. Fears. Memories. The three hit like lightning, and I hate the irrepressible terror that accompanies them. *Nothing happened to me. I don't need to live in fear.*

When I look up to see him in the doorway, one hand is on his hip in that way that tells me he's used to wearing his utility belt and holster. A smile is on his handsome face, and an adorable French bulldog named Disco is under his arm.

"Sorry. I knocked at the front. You didn't answer, but I saw your car was here and figured it was okay to come in."

Rubbing the spot on my head, I shove down my thundering pulse and smile shakily at Disco and the very attractive man holding him.

How'd I forget to lock the door?

My mind reels over my mistake. Over what if *he* came back.

"Des? You okay?" Jeff asks as he takes a step toward me, concern owning his expression.

"That's totally fine. I'm totally fine." The words are a rush of air as I try to hide my unease. "Here. Let me put the rest of these guys up for a sec before we set Disco down so I can introduce him to them one at a time."

"Yeah. Sure," he says as I grab a box of Milkbones to bribe the other dogs toward the back of the house where I have a dog room of sorts. It's painted in a bright yellow and has dog beds, water bowls, and dog toys. It's where I put the clean dogs after they're bathed and groomed.

When I come back to my grooming studio, he's nowhere to be found. "Jeff?"

"Coming," he says as his footsteps sound off in the hallway that leads to my kitchen and family room. "I set him down and he took off like he did last time. There's something about your kitchen he loves."

I grab Disco from Jeff and nuzzle the adorable dog. He grunts and groans as he always does. "I have a pot roast in the Crock Pot. He probably smells it."

"So what time am I coming over for dinner?"

I stare at Jeff. "We already tried that, remember?"

Both of our cheeks heat at the memory of our torrid few-week tryst, where we enjoyed the hell out of each other's bodies but agreed there wasn't much else between us. A relationship just how I like them—short, hungry, and over without any attachment.

"Yeah, but...sometimes it's good to take a walk down memory lane."

I push against his chest as he steps closer. "A walk down memory lane is one thing, but I assure you crawling up my thighs isn't where memory lane is located."

He laughs and shakes his head. "Can't blame a man for trying."

"Can't fault a woman for saying no."

We stare at each other for the briefest of seconds, each gauging if the other is being serious or if a quick relapse into each other would be worth it. It's been five months since I've had sex—with him no less—but I don't think need should dictate this decision.

This woman wouldn't complain about a good orgasm or three...but Jeff comes with ties—the kind of ties where he wanted more—and I don't like anything that binds me unless it's to my headboard in the pursuit of hot sex.

"I haven't seen you around lately. You hiding? You have a hot man you're using as a sex slave I should be worried about?"

"You applying for the job?" I laugh as his eyes darken and lips quirk up in a smile, and I realize the opening I just gave him. "I've been busy is all."

"Busy? Since when does busy stop you from letting loose? You're going to turn into a crazy cat lady pretty soon if you keep hibernating the way you are."

"I'm already the crazy dog lady, so does it really matter?" I ask to try and avert what he's really asking: *Are you okay? Are you worried you're going to run into him on the streets so you're hiding here instead?*

"Cats, dogs… The town of Sunnyville misses you." He chuckles. "Karaoke night down at The Tavern is boring without you."

"Yeah, yeah." I wave a hand at him like he's crazy.

"I'm serious." He takes a step forward and puts a hand on the side of my waist. "I've missed seeing you."

"Am I interrupting something here?"

We both jump back at the sound of Grant's voice in the doorway. "Jesus. It's like a cop convention in here all of a sudden," I say and take a step back from Jeff to look over his shoulder at my best friend's husband.

Grant is six foot plus, with dark hair and a great body. He's more than easy on the eyes and definitely smitten with my best friend, Emerson. But that little lift to his eyebrows, and glance from Jeff to me and back, is a simple question of *is something going on between you two?*

Leave it to a man to notice the obvious five months too late.

"Jeff was just dropping off Disco," I say, lifting the dog in my hands for emphasis.

"I was," he says, lips twisting and feet shifting. "Pick him up about what time?"

"Four-ish works. And if something happens and you get called to shift, he's more than welcome to stay till tomorrow."

"Sounds good." Jeff takes a few steps back with a smile on his lips to me and a soft nod and the word "Sir" on his lips to Grant.

We both stand in silence as Jeff's footsteps retreat and the front door shuts.

"Did you have to scare him off?"

"I'm his superior."

"I didn't see either of you in uniform, and I really don't need the big-brother routine."

"I don't have to wear a uniform anymore when I'm on the job."

"Smart-ass."

Grant fights a smile and shakes his head as we fall into our typical sibling-ish banter. He looks over his shoulder and then back to me. "He's a little young for you, don't you think?"

He might be young, but the boy has skills in the sack.

"And your point is…"

"Maybe that's why you never have a guy around for more than a few weeks."

"Maybe I like it that way." I curtsy and roll my eyes as we repeat the same conversation we've had a hundred times. "Not everyone wants what you and Em have."

"Uh-huh." He reaches out and pets Disco. "He's still too young for you."

"And young means he has stamina."

"Stamina is one thing, Des. Experience is another." His grin is wide and crooked, and there's that sex appeal Emerson fell in love with.

"Let me guess, this is where you inform me that you have experience in spades."

"I'll let Emerson tell you what I do or don't have because this is an odd conversation to have with you," he says through a laugh, cheeks flushing pink, discomfort all around. "What was he doing here?"

"Back to Jeff already? He was dropping Disco off. You're the one who sent him here in the first place, so if we were to accidentally fall into bed with each other—*again*—it'd be all your fault."

"*Again?*" He laughs. "Christ. TMI."

"Don't stick your nose where it doesn't belong, Officer Sexy," I say, referring to my immediate thoughts, and the nickname I gave him the first time we met a few years back.

"And I didn't send Jeff here."

"No? What about the twenty other cops who have shown up in the past few weeks, who never took an interest in getting their pets groomed before?" I roll my eyes and shake my head. "I'm supposed to buy that it's just a coincidence that suddenly they need Fido clipped and washed?"

"What can I say? You're building a reputation around town."

"And you're lying through your teeth. You know cops are too straight-laced for my liking." He just widens his smile while I glare. "You're frustrating."

"Thank you. I'm told that often."

"How's Em doing?" I know damn well she's the one who tells him that.

"She's good. You've probably talked to her more recently today than I have." He chuckles and is most likely right, but asking benign questions is better than having him look too closely.

Shit. He's looking too closely.

Turning my back to him, I set Disco on the floor before moving toward the washing station. I don't want to do this right now. I don't want him to see through the false pretense of *fine* that's hidden me for a while now.

"You're still not sleeping are you, Des?" His voice is right behind me when he speaks. He's not going to let me get away with putting him off.

"I sleep like a baby."

"Which means like shit. Did you forget the kids don't sleep for more than a few hours at a time?"

"It's an expression, Grant."

"Yeah...well...if the shoe fits?" His tight smile tells me he's not going to let this go like I want him to.

I hang my head in the silence that ensues. "I'm fine," I say.

"Fine as in you never think twice about what happened or fine as in it's all you think about and you don't want anyone to know?"

I take a deep breath, hating that his question is hitting too close to home. "Fine as in fine."

"I don't buy—"

"You know what? I'm sick of looking over my shoulder. Of being afraid of the dark. Of jumping when a customer comes into my business."

He gives me the second I need before he rounds to the other side of the wash station with Disco in his arms, licking the underside of his neck.

"It's going to take time."

Anger bubbles up inside me. "Time? Is that all it is, Grant? Time to get over the petrifying fear of waking up to a man standing over my bed? Because I don't know about you, but it feels like it's going to take a hell of a lot more than that to make it go away." Tears threaten—when I don't *ever* cry—and my teeth grind together as I try to shove unwelcome dark emotions and fear behind the façade of cheer I've been projecting these past few weeks.

"It's normal. What you're feeling is nothing to be ashamed of."

"Fucking great. Thanks for the psych eval."

"What's your problem, Des? Why is it so hard for you to admit that this has you rattled? It's perfectly okay to—"

"Perfectly okay to what?" I counter as I turn the water on and then off. I drop the sprayer in the sink, brace my hands on the side of the tub, and hang my head for a beat. I don't show emotion. I don't break down. I don't admit to anyone I'm scared...so why do I want to tell Grant when I haven't even admitted it outright to his wife?

It's because I'm sick of being tough and want things back to the way they were.

"Does it make you feel better to hear me admit I'm scared most nights? Is that what you want to hear me say?" I bite back my anger with the rising bile in my throat, hating that he's the only person who can get me to admit something like this out loud.

"No. It doesn't." His sigh is heavy, weighing down the space between us, despite the adorable puppy I should be cooing over.

"Any news on who it was or where he is?" I choke on the simple thought that he could come back.

"No." His eyes are serious as he sets Disco down and stares at me.

"I'm so stupid." I laugh, but there isn't an ounce of humor in the sound.

"You did nothing wrong."

"I wish you'd stop saying that to me. Obviously I did something to someone and they...I don't know what they did." My voice wavers. Hating hearing the sound, I add a touch of my typical sass to cover it up. "I mean, I get that most people are in love with me, but stalking takes it to a whole new level."

"It's not funny, Des. Nothing about this situation is."

"Yeah. Yeah. But how do I know this isn't on me? Have I met him at Hooligan's and accidentally led him on...so he's hurt?" *Would that justify why some stranger broke into my house and watched me sleep?* "Let's hope whoever it was got his rocks off and has now moved on to the next person." If I keep saying it, then maybe I'll believe it.

"We don't know enough to even say that, and regardless, Des, this isn't on you. He broke the law and is definitely high up there on the creep-factor record so...quit saying that, because it's not funny."

I pick up Disco and set him in the basin. "You'll be happy to know I've sworn off men from here on out."

"That's funny," he says and turns the water on for me.

"You doubt me?"

"I doubt a lot of things about you right now, but mostly that this isn't bugging you."

"It's not. I'm fine."

"I could get you a security guard if that would let you sleep better at night."

And draw more attention and more town gossip and more just everything I don't want?

"I started taking self-defense classes. Does that make you feel better and get you off my back?"

"You did? I know a guy who—"

"I did. Can we now get back to normal life where we don't have to talk about this every time I see you?"

He falls silent, and I hate that its return has me looking up to meet his eyes. "*Desi*." The compassion in his voice....*so goddamn sick of it*. My vulnerability turns into anger.

"Drop it, Malone." We wage a visual war of wills—where he wants to do his job to protect and serve, and I want to forget it ever happened. "Thank you for looking out for me, but he's long gone."

I hope.

Chapter Five

Reznor

"Oh my God. Logan is going to be here any minute and Pussy is soaking wet."

Well fuck if those words didn't grab my attention and snap me wide awake from where I was dozing off on the backyard porch swing.

Was I dreaming?

Desi Whitman.

Yes, *Whitman* because I looked on the roster to get her full name after thinking about her way more than I wanted to.

The voice sounded just like hers.

I must be dreaming.

"Of course. I never take care of Pussy, and the one time I do, she gets wet and messy before he gets here to take her home to play."

Now that? That definitely got my attention.

The damn swing creaks as I get up from it and head toward the side of the house to the left of me. The clapboard house where dogs are always barking and the sign that says Doggy Style over the garage door has frequently drawn my curiosity.

But I haven't looked in the few days I've been here. I'm not here to be a nosy neighbor, and fuck if I haven't been busy unpacking and cleaning up the place. Besides, I normally keep to myself, but when there's talk of a wet pussy, no man is going to stand idly by and let it be.

"I've stroked you"—*groan*—"and petted you"—*sigh*—"and trimmed all your fur to perfection, and this is how you repay me? By getting soaking wet and filthy before your daddy comes back to town?"

My smile is wide and I'm not gonna lie, my dick is stirring to life as I walk around the front of the house and peer down the side yard to see a woman's backside. She's on her hands and knees on the sodden grass, with mud coating her calves and hands. One mighty fine ass is pointing in my direction.

"You dirty girl, you," she mutters and I can't help but laugh. I've seen a lot of shit in the line of duty, but hell if I can remember hearing a woman talking to herself like this before.

"Excuse me? Is everything okay?" I ask, part caution, part curiosity in my voice, but I'm sure as shit not prepared for what I see when the woman sits up on her knees and faces me.

Desi Whitman.

A soaking-wet Desi with a white T-shirt smeared with mud and the dark pink of her nipples hinting beneath the fabric.

Nothing like a wet pussy and hard nipples.

"Oh my God. *It's you.*" She sneers with disdain as she jabs a finger my way and rises to her feet—irritation etched on her gorgeous face.

"Yep, last time I checked, I was me."

"What are you doing here?" Her eyes narrow and she throws her hands on her hips, not caring that she has now dirtied the sides of her shirt.

"I'd like to ask you the same question."

"I live here."

"Well...so do I." I hook a thumb over my shoulder toward the other side of the fence and watch as her eyes widen and her back straightens.

Why does it not surprise me that she's going to fight me even now? And why do I already know that this—*she*—is going to be a problem in more ways than one? I haven't forgotten what it felt like to have my hands on her for those eighty minutes last Thursday.

Or how sharp that tongue of hers is.

It's as though I *have* to goad her. *Have* to get a rise out of her.

She starts to speak several times and then thinks better of whatever venom she has on her tongue before starting again, only to fall into the same trap and then stopping herself, so instead I get her blank stare and unmistakable anger.

She's tall. At least five foot eight, with legs for days that paint a picture in my head of exactly what they should be wrapped around. She's pretty in a nonconventional way. A mixture of quirky and sexy instead of your classic beauty. Her blue eyes are big, her lashes long, and her lips are full and wide.

It takes me a second to remember the presence of mud and water everywhere, because her tits are right there, and hell if it isn't a damn fine sight.

And then I remember the wet pussy.

"Looks like you could use some help here," I finally say when I trust myself and take a step toward her.

"With what?" She lifts her chin in a show of defiance.

"I don't know. Either the mud since it looks like you might have a sprinkler leaking"—another bristling of her shoulders—"or I could always help you take care of that wet pussy of yours."

She clenches her fists. "You're an asshole, you know that?"

I chuckle to irritate her further. "And you're the woman going on and on about how you never take care of your pussy, and now it's trimmed and wet"—I shrug—"and since you went to all that trouble, don't you think someone might as well reward you?"

I dodge as she throws the rag in her hand my way. "Figures you'd think that way."

"I take that as a no, then?"

"No."

"Hey, I'm only going off what I heard. Only crazy people talk to themselves like that."

"Pussy is Logan St. Claire's precious cat. And Logan Sinclair is one of the assholiest people out there—"

"Is that even a word?"

"Even more so than you."

"Probably not," I say just to push her buttons.

My words stop her—surprise her—and she looks at me with a tilt to her head. Pieces of brown hair that have fallen out of her ponytail rest against her cheek.

"Yeah. You're right. You take the cake."

"Says the woman who insulted me in the first two minutes of our initial conversation."

"Glad I could leave a great first impression. Maybe you should have taken the hint and left me alone," she says, finding her footing beneath her again and letting that temper reignite.

"You only get one chance to make a first one..."

She huffs in response and out of the corner of my eye I see a mass of white fluff—or perhaps it used to be white fluff because now it's spotted in brown mud—skirt across the grass and into the open back door.

Pussy.

"Remind me not to like *him*."

"Like who?" she asks.

Gotta keep her on her toes.

"Logan St. Asshole," I say. "Guys who have cats—correction, guys who name their cat Pussy—either aren't getting any or are using the name as a way to state they're not gay when everyone already knows they are."

"Is that so?"

"Yep. Why be ashamed of who you are and hide behind a cat? Just live the best life."

There's something I say that has her head tilting to the side again. She takes me in a little longer than expected. "It's the former," she finally admits.

I shrug. "Why is he an asshole?"

"The bigger question is how is he not an asshole?" For the briefest of moments I see a ghost of a smile on her lips, and it reminds me of how pretty she was the other day before the defense class began when she was chatting me up.

"Doggy Style?" I ask.

"That's the name."

"But Pussy is a cat."

"You're quite observant..."

"I can imagine you attract all kinds of interesting folks with that name," I say, dismissing her sarcasm.

For the briefest of moments something flickers through her eyes and before I can put a finger on it, the emotion is gone, but it reminds me of what I saw in them the other day after class.

"Just as I'm sure you do working with SWAT."

"Always." I look at the cute cottage-style house. "You lived here long?"

We stare at each other in silence, and it's almost as if she remembers she isn't supposed to like me. Her expression and posture suddenly stiffen...probably because she realized she was smiling at me.

And fuck if I know why it turns me on.

"It's none of your business."

So that's how she wants to play it? Fine.

"Then it's also none of my business that Pussy ran into the house about two minutes ago." She narrows her eyes and sneers at me again. "It's your loss, Desi."

"What is?"

"That you don't trust me to show you just how good I am with something wet and groomed." And with that parting comment, I flash her a lightning-quick grin before heading to my side of the fence, while she grumbles and curses me out under her breath.

I hear her door slam.

I hear her call for Pussy again.

And all I can think about is how damn unexpected she is—and at the same time such a very welcome distraction.

I think I'm going to like my time in Sunnyville.

Chapter Six

Desi

The room is dark when I wake up.

My heart is racing and the *whoosh* of my pulse pounds in my ears.

I jump at the shadows in the room. At the sound of one of the dogs I'm watching scratch at something in his crate in the other room. At the sheets pulling off me when I move my feet.

Because all I can see is the sinister shadow over me when I woke up three weeks ago.

All I can feel is that unending panic of being alone and vulnerable.

All I can remember is that all-consuming fear that robbed me of my thoughts and paralyzed me from action as I sat there fully aware of everything around me—his scent, the harsh rasp of his breath, the complete control he had over me without saying a single word.

I know he's not here now.

Physically anyway.

But that's almost worse...*isn't it?*

Not hearing from him, not knowing where he is, *who he is*, is even scarier.

I stare at the ceiling for the longest time and try to make sense of the shadows, but just like every other night this week, sleep won't come. I know it's hopeless.

The dogs whine when my feet creak over the raised wooden floors of my house. I open their kennels and get lost in their kisses and attention as I try to figure out what activity I'll do tonight to occupy the hours when I should be sleeping.

I've already cleaned and scrubbed and reorganized every corner of my house and fear I've run out of things to do. It's the wee hours of the morning when you realize you're the loneliest—kind of like I feel right now.

"Do you guys have to go potty?" Tails wag and butts wiggle on the three dogs in response. "Okay. Let's go."

And then my steps falter a few feet before the back door as my mind runs through who could be out there. Whether *he's* waiting for me.

"Get a grip, Des," I mutter to myself. "Whoever it was got what he wanted and left." I stare at the doorknob and then at the shadows outside to see if any of them move. "Either that or you weren't hot enough for him to want."

I say the words but shudder.

Humor.

It's how I cope.

It's how I tell myself that it was nothing more than a man trying to break into my house, and when I woke up in the middle of his attempt it scared him off.

It's how I open the door to let the three dogs out, eager to relieve themselves.

And when I look to the right to where Reznor lives and see the lights burning bright in his house, I can't help but wonder what keeps him up at night.

Chapter Seven

Desi

Bang. Bang. Bang.

What the hell?

I must jump a foot off the ground. Thank God I'm not grooming a dog or else I'm sure there would be a very random strip of hair missing down its back. *Or worse.* A cut ear...

And then I slink behind the wall so I'm not in the line of sight of any of the windows.

Bang. Bang. Bang.

"Desi, it's Rez. Open up."

The sound of his voice has my panic morphing immediately from sheer terror to anger. I welcome the feel of my temper as it wipes out the exhaustion and panic, and I let it ignite as I stalk the few feet to the back door.

When I fling it open, Reznor is standing there with his arms folded over his chest, a baseball hat low on his forehead, and an irritated look on his face. The sun is fading behind the hills at his back, bathing the valley of Sunnyville in a soft glow, and I hate—absolutely hate—that my stomach flutters at the sight of him.

I'm not a flutter girl. I'm a *quick bang of lust between the thighs, it's time to go to the bedroom* type.

Flutters don't happen.

But I fluttered.

Crap.

"What?" I snap at him, trying to combat my unwanted attraction to him, when every part of my body reacts to him. To the rough cut of his jaw. The deep brown of his eyes. The slight curve of his smile.

"Good evening to you too." He chuckles.

"Ever heard of a front door?"

He looks at me for a beat before shaking his head. "Sorry. I thought that was the business entrance and this was the personal. I didn't mean to—"

"Scare me? Yeah. You did."

"Fine. Next time I'll knock so you know it's me."

"That's not what I mean—"

"Something like this," he says with zero regard for me telling him that there won't be a next time. He raps his knuckles on the side of the doorjamb: *knock-knock. Knock-knock-knock.*

His grin widens as he takes in the frustration on my face.

Yes, I'm being a bitch.

No, he doesn't deserve it.

But he made me flutter.

And he's him—looking all hot and sexy—and I'm me—a woman who has sworn off men for a while—and hell if the sight of him isn't getting things in me revved that I don't want him to hold the keys to.

"What? You don't like that pattern?" He angles his head to the side. "I can make a different one." He lifts his fist to knock.

"No, it's fine. It's just…" I blow out a sigh and hate that the shy smile on his lips looking like a little boy's, mixed with the tattoos decorating his arm are like kryptonite wearing down my defenses. "That pattern is fine."

"Good," he says as if he doesn't hear the annoyance lacing every syllable I speak.

Silence falls as we stare at each other for a beat as I figure out what to say and he waits for it.

"You didn't show up to class tonight."

Just when I thought I was starting to like him…

"I wasn't aware you were keeping tabs."

His eyes narrow as he looks closer than I want him to look before crossing his arms over his chest and leaning a shoulder on the doorjamb, forcing me to take a step back into the house to gain some distance.

"Why does the class scare you so much?" he asks.

"No one said it did."

"No one had to say it…your actions speak for themselves."

Once again he's caught me flat-footed—first with the damn flutters and now with wanting to know why I didn't show up to class. And I hate that I feel like I want to tell him when I don't talk about this with anyone other than Grant and Emerson.

But I don't. I recover quickly.

"I had to stay home. A plumber was coming to look at what I think is a broken pipe." He just looks at me, which prompts me to ramble further. "He didn't show up though."

He twists his lips as he judges whether to believe me or not.

"Is your water off?" he finally asks.

I nod, holding our gaze steady so he believes me, all the while feeling slightly let down that he's not pushing me more on this. "The sprinkler line is, yes. The grass is still wet, so I don't know...maybe it's the mainline. Maybe it's God knows what."

"He didn't show?"

"He's coming. He's running late. He'll be here later."

That's the problem with lying to your neighbor—they can see people coming and going at your house and lies can easily be proven or disproven.

"Uh-huh." He doesn't believe me. Those brown eyes of his say it but he doesn't speak the words. "Desi, what happened to you to—?"

"Why don't you sleep at night?" The question is out of my mouth before I even think through explaining why I know that.

His subtle startle would probably go unnoticed by most, but I see it. I notice the slight hesitation that tells me there's something there beneath the surface.

He smiles and shakes his head. "It seems like we both have something the other one wants to know about. How about that?" He lifts his brows in challenge and then takes a step back off the porch. "Later, Desi."

And with that I watch him walk out of my yard.

In fact, I walk through the house to the front to watch him out the front window. He walks across his front yard over to his motorcycle in the driveway and fiddles with something on it.

I close my eyes briefly and fight the urge to walk outside and tell him about the man...

But why?

Is it because I see someone who possibly fights internal demons too? Or is it because last week, even though I'd felt like his crash dummy at class, I'd also felt extremely...*safe?*

Chapter Eight

Desi

"I promise you pickles and almond butter don't go together, Em," I say into my cell as I pull into the driveway.

"This baby has to be a boy. I swear. This pregnancy is different than my others. I craved nothing with Gwen and Taylor. No weird foods. No constant sex. No—"

"No wonder Grant's walking around tired all the time." I laugh. "Let the poor man get some sleep."

"He's not complaining by any means."

"What man would?"

"Am I going to get to see you soon?" she asks, and the sound of her voice has me listening closely. Hormonal pregnant woman versus something is really wrong.

"You okay?"

"Yeah. I'm just worried about you—"

"I'm fine, Em."

"But you're avoiding me. Ever since the creeper in your house— you're dodging coming over, because you don't want me to look you in the eye and know you're scared," she says, and I don't say a word in response. "I've known you too long, Des."

"I'm fine," I say in exasperation.

"Then tell me the last time you let loose. What wild party did you crash or which bar in town did you shut down while dancing on the tables? Come on, give this old married and pregnant lady someone to live vicariously through."

I smile but it's vacant of all happiness as I think of the woman I usually am. The one who has stories to tell and men to confuse. Instead all I do is chuckle in response.

"There aren't any, are there? And you tell me not to be worried about you?"

"I'm just in a funk is all."

"No, you've put yourself in a funk. You tell me that you're fine when you're not. You tell me this creep being in your house hasn't affected you, and yet you're afraid to leave your house. You tell me you know you're not to blame for this, but you're afraid to be the you I know and go dance with some stranger in a bar just because he can sing the lyrics louder than you." She tsks.

"That's not it." But it is it. The damn man in my bedroom has scared the shit out of me. He's made me fear that I'll meet him face to face, maybe even share a drink with him, and I wouldn't even know it.

"That's bullshit and you know it."

"Em." Her name is a sigh. A plea.

"Then come have lunch with me."

Fuck.

"Okay. I'll find a light client day and let you know."

"And there you go hiding again."

"It's just...it's just hard to explain is all."

"No one said you had to, but ferreting yourself away in hibernation isn't good for your soul either."

"I promise you I'll let you know a good day," I say to get her off my back.

"You better...or else I'll come there and watch you shave dogs and then throw up when you do all the gross stuff you have to do with them—"

"I should have never explained to you what expressing an anal gland was like."

She gags on the other end of the phone and I laugh. "You burned my memory forever."

"Goodbye, Emerson."

"Don't avoid me, or else I'll sic the cops on you."

"Oh, please." *Her husband already has.*

"I'll make up a reason—a well check or something—because we all know how much you don't want that to happen."

"I'll send you a day that works. Happy?"

"Very."

"Love you."

"Love you too."

I open the garage door and get out of my car, preoccupied with the bags of groceries I'm carting inside. Once the rustling of the plastic settles as I set them on the counter, I hear it.

It's a distinct sound. One I can't place, so I stand completely still with my heart lodged in my throat to see if I hear it again.

It happens. The *thunk* of metal against dirt. The squish of sodden mud.

The curse muttered under a breath.

"What the hell…" My words fall flat when I fling open the back door to see Reznor in the backyard with a shovel in one hand, on his knees in a slew of mud, and said mud covering so many parts of him I can't see them all.

"This pipe is really a bitch. Whoever laid this sprinkler system needs to change careers." He looks over at me for a split second and then goes back to digging like it's completely natural that he's in my yard fixing my sprinkler system.

And I don't know how it makes me feel. On one hand, that means he noticed the plumber never showed—so that means he was watching…and I kind of like that he was watching. On the other hand, he just stepped into my life and took over, and I'm not sure I like that—the domesticity of it.

"What are you doing?"

"Fixing your sprinkler system," he says with a grunt as he shovels a scoop full of mud onto a tarp that's blanketing a corner of the back patio.

"But why?"

"It's broken, isn't it?" He's fiddling with a pipe, with the piece that connects them—or that looks like it connects them—and is putting some blue goop around the inside before joining them together. "I already fixed the damn thing once and then when I turned it back on, your pressure regulator wasn't turned right so it blew another fitting off. It's as if the guy forgot to glue the pieces together."

"I'm sorry."

"Not your fault."

"But, Reznor…why would you do this?"

"Because I'm a nice guy? Because you had your water off, and I didn't want your flowers to die?"

I snort, not buying it for a second.

"What? You don't believe me?" he asks as he takes a second to look my way behind his tinted lenses. He has mud smeared on his cheek and sweat running down his temple as he holds the pipe, but the slight smirk tells me my hunch is right.

"Why are you fixing my sprinklers?"

"So you wouldn't have an excuse to miss class next time." The smile he flashes me is as bright as the sun beating down on him and without saying another word, he turns back to the muddy trench and glued pipe and everything that is not me.

I should be pissed at him. I should tell him that no one tells me what to do or where I need to be. Instead I watch him. I stand and study him from my back stoop as my mind whirls over what to do about this man who has single-handedly pushed his way into my life and thoughts.

I have groceries on the kitchen counter that need to be put away. I have bills I need to pay. I have clients to call back, and yet I don't move, unwilling to tear my eyes away from him.

"It's a lot easier to talk to me than to have me try and read your mind, you know," he says, breaking through my thoughts.

"Maybe I don't like to talk." I lie.

His chuckle tells me he doesn't buy it. "The first time we met you talked a mile a minute without much prompting, so sell me a lie I might actually believe."

"How about you're irritating?"

That grin is back, and so is the damn flutter when he stands to full height from his spot in the mud. "That's not a lie." He looks back to the pipe, and without saying a word, strips his sodden shirt over his head and balls it in his hands. My eyes go to his chest. How can they not when I clearly remember the feel of those muscles etched in his torso as they moved against mine in class the other day?

Whew. They sure know how to make them good in the SWAT team.

When he turns to me, I'm sure he catches me taking a look—what woman wouldn't?

Besides, I missed my chance to stare at him before. This time I'm going to enjoy the view.

His whole left shoulder, pec, and arm down to his wrist are covered in a dizzying array of designs and images. Color fills some, while others are shaded or left outlined. I take in the taut stomach muscles, the various scars hinting across his torso, and then the intensity in his eyes when I scrape my gaze back up his torso to meet his again.

"Yes?" he asks.

"What are your tattoos of?"

"A little bit of this. A little bit of that," he says nonchalantly as he takes a few steps my way. "We all have our stories to tell. Some of us choose to put them on display for those who look close enough to decipher."

"Hmm," I murmur. Strangely, I *want* to look closer to know his story and yet don't want to give him the satisfaction of knowing that I want to. He's pushy, arrogant...but he's here fixing my sprinkler because he cares whether I'm in class. *He cares.* "I figured you were trying to cover up old war wounds."

His chuckle is soft. "I've got too many of those to cover up." He moves beneath the patio cover, leaving a muddy trail with each footstep, and his undeniable energy sucks up the air in the small space between us. I slide my eyes back to his.

"I didn't notice."

His smile toys at the corner of his mouth. "You noticed."

"No, actually, I didn't." My spine stiffens as the flutter reappears when he reaches out without any thought to the mud covering his hands and places his finger under my chin to lift it so he can study me.

"What I can't figure out about you, Desi Whitman, is why you keep trying to pretend you're not interested when you clearly are?"

"That ego of yours is going to be sore tomorrow."

"Why's that?" he asks.

"It's working out right now, flexing its muscles and doing some heavy lifting." It's pretty damn hard to be sarcastic when the man still touching you is making you want to lean in and kiss those sexy lips of his and prove just how right he is.

And just how wrong you are.

A sheepish smile paints his lips. "Ah, but you like the muscles."

I like a whole lot more than the muscles.

"Mmm." It's all I trust myself to say.

He leans in closer. I can feel his breath feather over my lips and the look in his eyes—one that says his interest is as strong as mine: hungry and aroused as hell—is enough to make every part of me want to step forward and into him.

But I don't.

I want to.

But I also want to slow down whatever the hell this is.

"Hey, Desi," he murmurs as he leans in close enough that both of our eyes flicker down to the other's lips as we breathe the same air.

"Hmm?"

"You look gorgeous in that color."

Oh shit.

I just swooned.

First flutters.

Now swooning.

Both are things I never do.

"Thank you." My voice is barely audible when I finally swallow around the lump of desire clouding in my throat.

"For?" he asks, the rumble of his voice a seduction all in itself.

"For fixing my sprinklers."

"And?"

"And for the compliment."

His tongue darts out to wet his lips. "No need to thank me."

Time feels like it slows as we stand like this in the afternoon sunlight on my patio—me in a bright yellow sundress and him in mud-soaked jeans. The birds chirp above. My heart pounds in my ears. My nipples harden in anticipation.

Jesus, just kiss me already, will you?

"Desi?"

"Yeah?"

Just as I get my synapses to fire and lean in and take the initiative myself, he takes a step back and says, "I need to take a shower."

I draw in a shaky breath as his eyes remain on mine and their corners crease with his smile.

"It's a good look for you though." *Nice recovery, Des.* At least outwardly it is, because inside I'm kind of a wreck with more *want* than I care to admit to.

"I don't need to have mud on me to get dirty."

He winks, gives me one last once-over with eyes that relay every single thing they want to do to me, before he turns on his heel and heads in the direction of his house.

Unlike last time, though, I don't walk inside and sneak a peek at him. Instead I walk to the side of the house and watch him as he retreats. The strong lines of his back. The broad span of his shoulders. The sexy swagger that says he's a man who knows what he wants.

Jesus, take the wheel, because if I'm the one steering it, I'm going to drive right up on that stick shift and see how good he can change gears.

"Later, Desi Whitman," he says as he rounds the fence without looking back.

"Later, Reznor Mayne," I mutter to myself. I stare at where his very fine ass turned the corner to his house.

I shift to abate the ache everything about him has brought to life between my thighs.

He already has me feeling spent when we haven't even kissed yet.

But we will.

No doubt about that.

There's nothing wrong with admitting it to myself. We're two healthy adults. Two sexual beings. Two people who just made *come-fuck-me* eyes at one another so I'd say are definitely attracted to each other.

Christ, Des. Sleep with the man and get it over with already.

If it were only that easy. Because a part of me feels like sex with him wouldn't be enough. I wouldn't be satisfied. Hell, I pushed Jeff away to spare his feelings—I didn't want more. I've sworn off men altogether. Yet I'm sitting here thinking about Reznor. About his easy charm and cocky attitude and hot body.

And how he seems to see beneath the surface in a way I don't let anyone else and yet he doesn't push or call me on my bullshit façade of courage. But he still seems to want me.

Sleep with him. Then you can move on.

The problem is I don't think moving on would be starting something I'm not certain I'm ready to handle.

Chapter Nine

Reznor

The beer is cold and shocks the nightmare and memories from my mind. The squelch of the radio. My command authorizing the breach echoing over it. The pop of the flash bang. The crack of the gunshots. The echoes of the screams.

I tilt the bottle up and keep drinking until it's empty.

It doesn't even taste good, and it sure as hell doesn't wash the taste of guilt away. Nothing seems to these days.

Thunder roars in the distance as heat lightning flashes through the sky. Dogs bark somewhere in the neighborhood beyond and the sound tells me I fell asleep and forgot to close the windows.

Toto, we're not in San Francisco anymore.

There's no way I would've forgotten to do something like that at home. Never. But despite the nightmare I'm slowly coming down from, I do feel more relaxed here. Case in point, the open windows.

"You okay?"

When I hear Desi's voice, I don't jump. Years of on-the-job training have settled my nerves, but I question why I didn't know she was there.

Am I losing my edge?

Then again, maybe I did sense she was there. Maybe she's who I was standing here looking out into the darkness thinking about. Maybe she's the one I want to lose myself in for a bit to forget and feel good and everything in between.

"It's three in the morning," I say as I walk to the screened-in porch and open the door for her, although the fact that she's here tells me she was going to open it herself anyway. "What are you doing here?"

She doesn't speak at first but rather stands there and studies me. There are dark smudges beneath her eyes like I'm sure there are under mine. Her hair is piled on top of her head in some kind of messy bun and her face is bare of makeup. Her long legs are bare apart from very short shorts and her bright orange tank top leaves nothing and everything to the imagination.

Christ, she is sexy.

I clear my throat and love how her eyes drag over every inch of me just like I have imagined her hands would. I should offer to put some shorts over my boxer briefs. I should ask her to come in. Hell, I should do a lot of things but somehow it seems fitting we meet like this.

Somehow I already know how this will end.

And as much as I'm here in Sunnyville to get my head screwed back on straight and uncomplicate everything, I'm not going to fight it one damn bit.

"Desi?"

"I heard you shout. The dogs got restless. I don't know…" For a woman I've yet to see hesitate, her uncertainty tells me all I need to know. *She's as interested as I am.* She looks at the fingers she's twisting together before looking back at me. "I wanted to make sure you were all right."

"What were you doing up, Desi?"

The half-smile she gives turns me on more than it should. It's part sheepish, part minx, and whole lot of projected suggestion.

"Couldn't sleep." Another aversion of her eyes taking a quick sweep of my place. "You?"

"Nightmare."

"You okay?" She takes a step inside for the first time, and the sexual tension between us begins to spark in the static of the air.

"Been better." I reach out to tuck a loose piece of hair behind her ear.

"Wanna talk about it?"

"Not really," I murmur as my fingers cup the side of her face, and I run my thumb over the softness of her lips. "You?"

"No."

Thunder rumbles, but I can still hear the hitch of her breath as I slide my hand from her jaw to her shoulder and trace the dent between her collarbones.

"What are we doing here, Desi?"

The quick dart of her tongue to lick her lips is enough to have my dick begin to stir to life. That's a lie. It already was stirring, but fuck if I'm not hard now.

"You're going to kiss me and make me forget my bad dream, and then I'm going to kiss you back to help you forget about yours."

"Is that so?" I murmur as I step into her so our bodies are barely touching. Just enough to turn me on further and not enough to make me question my next move.

"It is."

"What if I don't want you to kiss me?" I ask.

I jolt when her hand runs over my cotton-clad cock. Then I groan when she cups her palm over it and grips ever so lightly. "This tells me you're lying."

"You might be right."

Chapter Ten

Desi

He tastes like beer and sex and urgency.

And he looks like how I feel. Tired. Horny. Lost in a sea of wanting to forget. Desperate for the human connection we can each bring the other.

Those were my first and only thoughts when his lips met mine and began their exquisite assault on my senses.

There was no softness, no tenderness—just stripped-down necessity in that first kiss. And the one that followed after that. And the one that is still ongoing as his hands begin to roam up and down the curves of my body. There is no hesitation as they slide beneath the hem of my tank, igniting my skin with the soft scrape of his fingertips against my lower back.

My hands find him too. Up the ridged plane of his chest. Over the strong muscles in his shoulders. To the back of his neck where I thread my fingers through his hair and urge him closer so I can show him how much I want him.

But nothing our hands can do at this moment rivals the conviction of our kiss. He's a mixture of raw need and desperate desire, and I try to match him kiss for kiss—lick for lick—nip for nip—each touch feeding our urgency to take more from the other. To demand more from the other.

We are chaos as we bump into the wall at my back. All hands and lips and groans and moans, but when he presses my body there, when his hardened dick taunts me in the most deliciously torturous of ways, I know if he's not going to speed up the process, I sure as hell am.

My hand is back on his cock. It slips beneath his waistband, down past the bristle of hair, and wraps around the smooth, cool hardness of his dick. His body stiffens and he groans against my lips as my fingers play over his length.

Everything about the moment—the feel of him, the sound of him, the air around us that smells one hundred percent of him—only serves to deepen my desire.

And that means I want him now.

I don't want to think about the flutter or the swoon or how I've sworn off men, because right now my body is on fire for his and has thrown caution—that I know will be back shortly—to the wind.

"Reznor," I murmur against his lips before I rub my thumb over the crest of his cock. I smear precum around as his hand cups my breast and does the same motion over my nipple. "I want—"

He smothers my words with his lips. He silences my request when he touches his tongue against mine. His hands skim down my torso and cuff mine that are pleasuring him.

"No."

"Rez—"

His chuckle against my lips is laced with so much intention that if I weren't already aching for him, I definitely would be now. "You'll get it all right, but like you told me, you only get one chance to make a first impression...and hell if I don't plan on impressing the hell out of you, Desi."

My eyes must widen or my body must stiffen or hell if I know, but I only see his eyes daring me to challenge his statement. I only hear our ragged breaths highlighted by raindrops beginning to fall outside.

He wets his lip with his tongue as a ghost of a smile paints his mouth.

"We don't need this anymore," he murmurs as he reaches for the hem of my tank top. I raise my arms as he pulls it off. When it clears my face, I love how his eyes widen in pure male appreciation.

"No?"

"No."

And this time when he steps into me and meets my lips, it's slow and soft. Sure there's hunger beneath the surface, vibrating to show me this tempo is as difficult for him as it is for me. But while our previous kisses were like a Molotov cocktail thrown at me already on fire, this kiss is like a slow-burning ember that's just starting to ignite. My body warms bit by bit, from the center out to my fingers and toes.

With his hands still cuffing my wrists, the focus is solely on our kiss.

On the connection of our tongues. On the finesse of his skill.

His lips coax me, brand me, warn me of the promise of what is to come. I already know without a doubt I'll take whatever he is going to give me. *I've not known this sort of...need before.* But I want him.

God yes, I want him.

Whereas before I wanted to rip his boxers off and get to the good stuff, the way he's pouring everything into this kiss—as if this is the end game—makes me want to melt into him and realize that this *is* the good stuff.

This is...the flutter and the swoon and every damn thing between.

It's intimate. *Reverent.* Everything I shy away from and tell myself I don't ever want.

But damn if it isn't all-consuming.

Lightning flashes and thunder roars. Enough to shock us apart and snap me from the spell I never agreed to fall under.

Our eyes meet across the darkened room and I see the desperation in his gaze. It looks the way I feel.

"Fuck me, Reznor."

That chuckle again. The one that feels like it rumbles through me deeper than the thunder does as he loosens the grip on my wrists and slides his hands between my thighs.

I sigh. I step farther apart. I dig my nails into his shoulders as he cups me and runs his finger up and down the length of my slit on the outside of my shorts.

"I never thought you'd ask," he says, moments before his lips crash back against mine and his fingertip slides beneath the hem of my shorts and finds me wet and wanting and oh-so aroused.

The next few moments feel like the lightning flashing around us. Unpredictable. Energetic. Explosive.

Clothes are removed in the short seconds that our bodies separate before they crash back together again. Stumbling steps are taken down a darkened hallway. His mouth is on mine. His hands are running over me. His body is against mine.

And this is how we fall onto his bed—in a torrent of unsated desire where we can't get enough. A rush of words falls from our mouths.

Please. Hurry. *Yes.* You ready? *Oh, God.*

Then there is nothing but pleasure as Reznor licks his fingers and rubs them up and down the length of me before using the crest of his dick to do the same. And then with eyes focused between my thighs and his tongue just barely between his lips in concentration, he pushes that glorious cock into me.

All words turn to groans.

All muscles tense and liquify as the pleasure of him sliding across my G-spot hits me.

"Reznor." It's a moan. A plea. A thank you.

"God, that feels good."

I nod—at least I think I do—because I'm too busy absorbing the pleasure assaulting me as he pulls out before taking his time to push back into me.

My hands grip the sheets as he palms my breasts when he starts to move with a bit more force. Driving in, grinding against my pelvis, ever-so-slowly pulling out before starting the frenzied process all over again.

The pace picks up. Our own panting and the sound of our bodies connecting with each thrust battling for an audience over the thunder.

Right there.

"Feel good?"

Oh yes.

"Jesus, woman."

He looks incredible as the muscles in his neck strain and his fingers dig into the sides of my hips as he tips my center to meet him with every thrust. A damn Adonis giving me exactly what I need.

And then it hits me.

The Molotov cocktail.

Its impact turning into an out-of-control wildfire.

It eats the oxygen in the room. It pushes and pulls at every part of me until the flames consume me in an explosion of pleasure.

The orgasm washes over me. In a tsunami of sensations. Followed by waves. Then ripples. With his hips stilled, he stares at me and watches me absorb the ecstasy.

Every part of me wants to look away, but hell if those eyes on me only heighten the intensity. It makes me want to show him how good he made me feel.

So I reach between my thighs where he's still hard and testing all restraint by not moving. I slide my fingers around the portion of him not buried within me.

He groans. His head falls back and his mouth falls lax as I guide him deeper into me before moving my hands to his hips to tell him I'm all his.

With a scrape of my fingers over his torso, his control snaps. His desire to give me what I need met, his own need supersedes all else now.

He slams into me. Harsh and ragged and desperate. His hands on me.

His eyes on me. His cock into me.

And within moments, it's my name that fills the room. It's his storm that takes over until his tense body relaxes and he drops onto the bed beside me.

Our ragged pants fill the room only to be rivaled with my pulse pounding in my ears.

"Holy shit." I finally laugh.

"You can say that again."

We fall into silence, our minds lost to what just happened between us. Mine wondering how I'm going to walk away unscathed, because Reznor Mayne is definitely a man I'd take seconds with.

But then again...I can't put my finger on it but this feels so very different than anything I've had of late. And late meaning in the past year or so...I may like to have my fun, but that doesn't mean I sleep around.

I hear the raindrops outside for the first time. The *tap, tap, tap* against the roof overhead through the open windows.

It had to be the eye contact.

Tap. Tap. Tap.

Or his need to slow it down and make a first impression.

Tap. Tap. Tap.

He reaches over and puts his hand on my waist.

Tap. Tap. Tap.

He starts to pull me over to him, and I have a slight panic attack.

I sit up instantly and shove to the end of the bed. "I...uh...I have to go."

"Desi?"

Without responding, I stand in the darkened room and pretend to look for my clothes on the floor when I damn well know they are in the other room. It's easier to look at the floor than him, but it does nothing to distract me from noticing the air smells like rain on the pavement and the sex we just had.

Like *us*.

I walk out of the bedroom without responding and hate when his feet pad on the floor behind me.

"What's going through that complicated mind of yours?"

I want you. I only just had you, but it isn't enough.

I find my shorts and pull them on as my mind frantically tries to shut out the butterflies beginning to dance. I'm not sure if they're there because I already want him again or because I know I can't have him.

That's not how I do things.

This isn't how I do things.

"Desi?" A little harsher, his sculpted body a silhouette against the sliding glass door at his back.

"I just—I heard the dogs barking. I need to take them out. I need...some of them get scared by thunder and I need to—" I stop, knowing that my excuse sounds just like what it is—an excuse—and yet I don't do anything to correct it. "I need to make sure I shut the back door. They'll run through it. Escape. I can't lose dogs I'm supposed to be taking care of."

His head is angled to the side as he watches me yank my tank top over my head, but I can't see his eyes.

Oh, how I want to see his eyes.

His sigh fills the room. "I'll walk you home—"

"No. It's fine. I'll be okay." That means a kiss goodbye, and I can't swoon right now when my insides have turned to mush and are already in a puddle at his feet.

It takes a second for me to find my flip flops and without looking his way, I mutter "Good night" like the chicken I am before walking out the door.

The screen door slams behind me as the rain hits me with each step through his backyard and into mine.

I thought I'd be able to breathe once I was outside of his house—when I was away from the scent of us together—and now it feels harder to draw in a breath.

It's because the sex was good.

At least that's what I'll tell myself.

That's my story, and I'm sticking to it.

Right up until I jog up onto my own porch, hair and clothes now plastered to my body, and yelp when Reznor's hand flashes out to my bicep and spins me around.

Without a word, his lips find mine again. He's instantaneously heat and desire as his tongue touches ever so briefly against mine and my arms fall lax to my side, afraid to betray my mind and grab on to him for one more round right here on the wet patio.

When we break from the kiss and he steps back, his eyes meet mine. He shakes his head ever so slightly. "There. Now you can go. Good night, Desi."

And it's only when he turns around to walk away that I realize he's still buck naked.

And I'm royally screwed.

Chapter Eleven

Reznor

The coffee scalds my tongue, but it's worth it in the morning silence. The still air is filled with birds chattering and somewhere in the distance a rooster crows. The jingle of dog collars and sharp nails on wooden floors can be heard from where I sit, and I notice how last night's rain washed away the mud from yesterday where it fell off the tarp and onto the concrete.

The door opens and dogs bound out of the house to the grass area. She appears shortly behind them in a different outfit from last night—but one that has me thinking about how her tits lifted with the fabric when I pulled her tank over her head.

Shit.

So many things I've relived about last night and yet I'm sitting here. I'm waiting for her. I'm wondering what the hell is going on.

The dogs—one black, one multi-colored, one with only three legs—do their business, but it's only when she turns to go into the house that she sees me sitting in the chair in the far corner of her porch.

Her yelp fills the air and her hand flies up to her chest. "What are you doing here?" she asks. But there is something in her eyes—genuine fear—that makes me think her being startled has to do with so much more than me surprising her.

"Sorry," I murmur and then knock on the table in the pattern I established earlier. *Knock-knock. Knock-knock-knock.* "Hi, it's me."

She huffs out a breath and rolls her eyes. "So?"

"Just enjoying my morning coffee," I say in a slow, steady drawl as her eyes narrow, and she tries to figure out what's really going on. "The dogs were good, then?"

She walks over slowly and takes a seat opposite me as the dogs come to greet me. I take my time giving them love so she can wonder more, and when the dogs go back to explore the yard and leave us be, I return my attention to my coffee.

When the waft of her shampoo or body spray or whatever the hell it is hits my nose over the dark roast, last night comes rushing back—not like it was far from my mind. The taste of her skin. The feel of her pussy. The sound of her moaning my name.

The panic in her voice when she jolted out of bed afterward.

"My job is interesting most days," I begin and see her stiffen in attention out of the corner of my eye.

"Self-defense?"

I snort a chuckle. "Nah. SWAT." I think about everything I'm missing by being here. Am I missing it or do I miss the chaotic normalcy and unpredictability? "Some weeks it's neverending boredom. Hour after hour. Day after day. Sitting and waiting for the next call, the next crazy person, the next whoever needs our help. Other weeks, we can't even put our weapons in their lockboxes before the next call comes in."

"It sounds—"

"Exciting? Daunting? Unconventional?" I ask as she nods cautiously, inquisitive eyes cast my way. "You could say that."

"I'm sure you've seen more than most people could ever imagine."

"Pretty much." I bring the mug to my lips. For some reason, I wish there was a little something stronger in it...when that's not something I've wanted in a long time. "It's all about control."

"What is?"

"My job." *My life*. "Who has it. Who wants it. How to transfer it from one person to another with the least amount of damage to everyone involved."

"It's a power play."

"Most times, yes."

I look her way and the barrage of questions normally thrown at me are in her eyes: Do you ever burn out? What's the worst you've seen? Have you ever been injured? And on and on...but she doesn't ask. She sits there with patient eyes and a soft smile, waiting for me to talk.

"I don't sleep at night, Desi, because every time I close my eyes I picture things I don't want to see."

"Rez—"

"A call went bad a few weeks ago. A hostage situation where kids were involved. I made the call to breach the house. Instead of the suspect taking his anger out on my team—shooting *at us*—he killed his kids, because he didn't want us to give them back to their mother."

"Christ."

"Nah, he wasn't anywhere in sight that day," I murmur as my mind takes me back to everything I see when I try to sleep. The hazy smoke in the air. The spray of blood on the wall from where my guys engaged and took the suspect out. The tears welling in Bull's eyes when he came out of the side bedroom and shook his head because the kids were gone.

"Those poor babies. My God. What animal would—"

"People do all kinds of things under the wide-reaching blanket of love."

"That's not love."

"Not how I see it, it isn't."

"I don't know what to say."

"There's nothing you can say. It was just a shit situation. A decision I'll second-guess for a long time. Should I have waited him out or would it have ended up with the same result regardless?"

"So that's why you're here?"

"More or less," I say and take a sip of my slowly cooling coffee. "I needed a change, something to clear my head for a bit."

"You're going back then?"

"Eventually. I think." I chuckle and run a hand through my hair. "Two months ago, if you would've asked me if I could see myself sitting in a slow, quiet wine town without going stir-crazy, I would've told you that you were the crazy one...but it's been a good change of pace."

"Sometimes change is good for the soul."

Our eyes meet as the dogs play in front of us, and we stare at each other in silence. "That's why I was up last night," I say then pause. "You?"

"Seriously?" She laughs, and I can see the change instantly. The stiffening of her spine and playing down of the fear I saw in her eyes when she found me sitting on her porch.

"Yep. Seriously. I'm trained to notice things, Des. How you jump when someone doesn't announce themselves. The fear and panic you get in your eyes. The self-defense class. It's written all over—"

"Maybe it's none of your business." Oh, there she is. Defiant. Fearless. Stubborn. "I don't need a hero swooping in to save the day."

My chuckle is raw and real. "I'm far from a hero, but I'd try to nonetheless."

"It's nothing. Leave it be," she warns.

"Maybe it isn't. But you wanna tell me what was up last night?"

"You were." She cracks the joke, but I don't give her the smile she's working for. Instead I give her my investigator's stare and wonder if she knows what she looks like right now. Like a teenager caught in a lie who isn't sure what to say and knows that no matter what comes out of their mouth, it will land them in hot water in one way or another.

"Desi…"

"I told you, I needed to check on the dogs."

"And I wasn't exactly done with you yet," I murmur and love the sudden catch of her breath that she tries to pretend didn't happen. Her eyes widen and she licks her lips as she tries to think of what to say. "Yeah, I wasn't. Not in the least. I had a few other ways to make you *tired*…but your loss."

"There are things we didn't talk about. Things that I don't—I'm not someone who commits—who—"

"Perfect. I'm all for casual-neighborly sex." I fight my grin, but lose the battle as I rise from my chair and move to rest my ass on the table so I'm directly in front of her. If she's going to bullshit me, she's going to have to look me straight in the eyes when she does it.

"That's not what I meant."

"Then what did you mean?" I fold my arms over my chest.

"I'm not a relationship girl."

"Good thing I didn't ask for one, then."

She's not getting out of this one as easily as I let her out of telling me her other truth. No way. No how.

I want the woman again—would have her right now if she let me—but something tells me there's a lot more beneath the surface I've yet to find out…and hell if I'm not determined to uncover it.

"That's not what I mean—"

"You keep saying that. And I keep waiting for you to explain what it is you do mean."

"If you'd back up and give me some space, maybe I could think straight."

I do the exact opposite. I step forward, put my hands on both arms of her chair, and lean down so we're face to face. "Maybe I don't want you to think straight. Maybe I know that's when you'll be the most honest. We slept together, Desi Whitman. It was incredible…*you* were incredible…and I'd like to do it again with you real soon…but I need a little more from you than a wham-bam-get-the-hell-out-ma'am. That's not my style. Far from it…"

"Maybe I'm just a one-night-stand girl."

"First of all, you're far from a girl." I drag my eyes up and down the length of her body. *No man would be satisfied with one night with Desi. She's gorgeous, passionate…fucking hot.* "Secondly, I'm all for a one-night stand…if I'm not going to see the person again, but I'm going to see you. I plan on seeing you…so yeah, I don't think that kind of parameter is going to work for me."

"Reznor—"

"Don't bother giving me your excuses," I say as I lean down and brush my lips to hers. Fuck if it isn't brutal to stop at a measly kiss from the woman who seems to harden my dick with just that. "Just practice saying *yes.*"

And with that, I stand to full height, smirk with a shake of my head, and walk out of her yard—this time with clothes on—leaving her and her stunned expression to think about the word yes.

The woman is scared.

And it's not only of strange men surprising her on her patio.

She's scared of someone getting close to her. *Emotionally, definitely.* Physically, maybe…unless, it seems, she gets to set the rules. A woman like Desi Whitman shouldn't live in fear. That carefree laugh of hers needs to be heard. So is that why I did that? Is that why I can't keep the fuck away from her when clearly she keeps trying to set boundaries?

Christ, Rez. Quit playing the hero. *She didn't ask you to be one.*

Pausing at the steps of my porch, I look over at the fence that separates our yards and shake my head. Whether she asked me to or not, it seems I'm putting on the cape regardless.

If she thinks she's done with me, she has another think coming. I'm making it my job to erase that look from her eyes.

Chapter Twelve

Reznor

"You got broken pipes?"

I lift my head up and see Grant peering at me down the cereal aisle of the grocery store. "My pipes are doing just fine, Malone." I laugh. "And what the hell are you talking about?"

"You're in a fishbowl now, Rez. Someone told the cashier at 7-Eleven that she saw the cute new guy with the tattoos and muscles at Ace Hardware buying some PVC. The cashier was at the coffee shop, and I overheard her tell it to someone else...so I drew some conclusions."

"Fucking great. Let's hope I don't go to buy some condoms. That'll really get the gossips going."

Note to self: Buy more condoms. My current stash isn't going to last if I'm living next door to Desi.

Then again, she needs to say *yes*.

"If you buy condoms, you'll have women lining up at your door asking for directions..."

"You mean the *take off your clothes, get on all fours* type of directions?" I ask with a chuckle.

"Something like that."

"How's work?"

"Same ol'. You know how it goes—feast or famine. Right now, it's feast."

"Running ragged, huh?"

"Pretty much. We're looking for a few more guys." He lifts his eyebrows and smirks. "You know, if you fall in love with it here and want to stick around."

"I'm not falling in love, no worries there," I say and wink but am shocked that my mind immediately veers to Desi.

Get a grip, Mayne. It was sex. One night.

A night I plan on having again and again.

"You never know," he says and shakes his head. "I wasn't falling in love either...and then it fucking hit me the minute I saw Emerson."

"Someday," I say. "Not now." I chuckle as I grab a box of Crispix off the shelf. "Right now I'm relegated to letting women beat me up in defense class and fixing broken sprinkler pipes for the hot neighbor."

"Hot neighbors are never a bad thing. Where you living?"

"What? You know I'm fixing pipes but not where I live?"

"I'm sure the cashier could have told me if I'd asked," he says with a laugh.

"I'm renting a house over on Vintage Road."

"Great area. We have a close friend who lives there. Desi Whitman."

I cough over the automatic laugh when he says that. "No shit," I finally manage.

"Something tells me you've met."

I nod slowly. "She's in my self-defense class," I admit, because if this is a small enough town that people are talking about what pipe I'm buying, they'll sure as hell talk about who's in the self-defense class.

"Really? She wouldn't happen to be the hot neighbor too, would she?" he asks, but there's something about my reaction that he catches. Leave it to a cop to notice everything.

"She's hot all right." I whistle low and appreciatively.

He laughs. "She and my wife are best friends. Have been since way before we met."

"Small world."

"It is indeed." We stare at each other, two men who understand the silent warning the other one is giving after the unspoken acknowledgement, that yes, I have slept with her.

His warning is *be careful.*

Mine is *it's none of your business.*

"It's actually quite a good thing. I can breathe a bit easier knowing you're next door after what happened."

If he didn't have my attention before, he sure as hell has it now.

I fight the need to know and the want for her to tell me herself. The need to know wins.

"What's that?"

"She hasn't told you?"

"Nah, but I know something's up. She jumps at the slightest sound. She's constantly on edge. Unsettled. The look is the same one any of us on the job have seen before. She tries to hide it, but it's still there. Add to that, she's in my class. Reluctantly."

Grant angles his head to the side and stares at me, almost as if he's asking if he can trust me when he damn well knows he can.

"About a month back, she woke up in the middle of the night to a man standing over her bed." *The fuck?*

"What?"

"Yeah. Guy stood there, scared the shit out of her, and then took off without doing a thing." He shrugs in obvious frustration. "Rare for Sunnyville. Masked intruder. No forced entry—"

"Which means he had a key or she left the door open."

"She didn't leave it open. She's a stickler for the dogs under her care and is always afraid one might bolt."

"Did the dogs bark to alert her?"

"Nope. That's one of the many odd things. The dogs didn't bark. The guy didn't say a damn word. Didn't threaten her...he stood there and stared at her before taking off out the back door."

"Any leads?"

"She gets a lot of odd calls because of the business name but none that pan out. She had a guy she met online...nothing serious, but after a few dates he wanted more and she didn't." *Is it bad I love hearing this?* "The guy sent some weird shit to her so he's my bet. That and the fact he's disappeared off the face of the earth..."

"Huh." It's all I say as I replay his words.

"Yeah. She feels like she led him on. Unintentionally, mind you—but you and I both know how someone who's not all there is challenged with rejection—"

"Shit goes downhill fast."

"Pretty much. She feels she brought this on herself...or at least that's the story she's giving me to hide the fact that it scared the shit out of her."

"It's always hard for the tough girls to admit they're vulnerable," I murmur, thinking about her reaction in self-defense class. The constant jokes. The need to redirect away from her discomfort. Then to our conversation yesterday. The way she jumped when she saw me on her patio. Her refusal to tell me why.

"Always. It seems you might know her pretty well." I smile, because fuck if I'm going to hide it. Grant throws his hands up and laughs. "I don't want to know."

"Smart man."

A text alerts on Grant's phone, and he glances at it for a second. "Shit, I've got to go."

"We've got to stop meeting like this," I say and point to the groceries around us.

He laughs and reaches out to shake my hand. "We do. We need to actually make plans next time."

"It's a plan." Grant takes a few steps away and turns back, and I smile. "Don't worry, Malone. The warning has already been heard and yes, I'll look out for anything strange at her house."

His smile is quick. "Thanks, Rez. She's family."

"And the second warning was just given," I say through a laugh that matches his. He turns around and disappears at the end of the aisle.

I stare at the cereal in front of me but the boxes of Crispix and Frosted Flakes blur together as I think about what Grant just said.

How so many things make sense now.

Desi's jumpiness.

The distance she prefers to keep.

She has good reason to be fearful *and* guarded.

But not on my watch. Fuck. No.

Chapter Thirteen

Desi

My strangled cry makes the dogs yelp when I catch the shadowy figure hulking in my back door.

"Need a hand with those?"

"Jesus, Reznor. Don't you ever knock?" I snap at him as I lean against the counter, hand against my heart. I tell my body to stop shaking as the dogs greet him with wags and licks, when *I* want to greet him with a knee to the crotch for scaring me so bad.

Maybe not.

Maybe I want to greet him with licks too.

And that's the problem, isn't it?

"Oh, sorry. I'll get it one of these days," he says and flashes me that grin of his that says he's in no way sorry. Of course, it does funny things to my insides even while giving me heart palpitations. And when he lifts his fist and does his knock on the side of the door—*knock-knock, knock-knock-knock*—I just shake my head.

"Please. Make yourself at home," I say, turning my back to him and looking at the mess I have strewn all over the floor.

His footsteps behind me are followed by a long low whistle. "Now that looks like a project if I've ever seen one."

"IKEA is the devil," I mutter. I stare at the screws and wood and instructions—in Swedish—and whoever forgot to put the English ones in the box is probably laughing at me over a beer right now. "How a woman goes from spending her nights out on the town to putting together furniture is beyond me."

But it's not beyond me. I know the truth. I'm the one looking at every random stranger I meet on the sidewalk in town wondering if he's the person who was in my house. I'm the woman who can't even sit and have a latte at the Coffee House without wondering about the people around me.

He stifles a laugh, pulling me from my thoughts as he walks past me and squats down to inspect the million parts. "Should I even ask what this is supposed to be?"

"Fuck if I know," I mutter. Sitting on the floor, I'm immediately surrounded by fur-babies wanting my attention. After they settle and I'm nowhere closer to understanding what the hell to do, I pick up the instructions again to pretend I'm handy...when I'm most definitely not. "It's a wall unit." I wave to the bare wall on the opposite end of my grooming room. "It's a new house for my supplies and products I sell."

"Hmpf." He takes the directions from me without asking as he lowers his knees onto the floor and thumbs through each page slowly. "Where's your Allen wrench and Phillips head?"

"Phillips head?"

"The screwdriver that looks like it has a plus sign on the end."

"Oh, yeah. It's right here." I lift it up and he takes it from me. "Wait. What are—"

"Shh. Just let me work on it."

"I can handle it myself, thank you."

His eyes flash up to mine and his hands pause midway through lifting a melamine board. "Looks that way."

"I'm serious. I'm perfectly capable and like to do stuff like this."

"By all means then," he says and reaches toward me with the tools and wooden dowels in his hand. His eyes meet mine and challenge me to show him just that.

So I do. I take the tools and the dowels and then spend the next few minutes attempting to understand what I don't understand, my frustration only heightened knowing he's sitting there with Kiki, the Yorkie, sitting in his lap, both of them watching me.

I last a while before I'm challenged to make the drawers. It's when I stare at the diagram and the screws that all look the same in front of me, that he takes the instructions from me and says, "Let me," and I acquiesce.

And without another word other than being asked to hand him this or hold that, he begins to assemble the damn thing. Piece by painstaking piece.

His brow is etched in frustration as he picks up parts only to set them back down next to the twenty other parts that are almost identical save for one tiny notch you can't see unless you turn it a quarter to the right while holding it at a forty-five-degree angle.

But I like watching him work. I sit in silence and study him. His concentration. The way he picks up the beer I brought him by the neck and takes a swig of it while surveying the progress. The quick glances he gives me followed by the soft smile before he looks back at the cabinet. There's something very comforting about having him here when I'm used to being alone. When I usually *prefer* to be alone.

"Why are you doing this?" I ask.

He gives me another one of those glances but this time his hands still and he angles his head to the side for a beat before speaking. "I'm antsy," he says, his confession surprising me while he returns to building. "I'm used to being on call twenty-four/seven. Waiting for that alert to go off, to grab my 'go pack' and head off to someone else's nightmare to try and fix it." He grabs a screw and I love watching his hands as he uses them. "Now I have nothing to do. The quiet is hard for me at times. I asked for a break, and I got it...but that doesn't mean I don't miss my guys and the job in general."

"That has to be a hard adjustment."

He nods. "It is. And I also know that if I don't help, you'll have another excuse why you can't show up to class on Thursday."

My shoulders sag as irritation flames. "I should have known." I reach my hand out to try and get the tools back. I don't need this shit. "Reznor—"

"You need to be in class. Right? You paid, so why aren't you showing up?" He pulls the screwdriver out of my reach and stares at me. "I've seen your instructor and he's pretty kick ass...it wouldn't be him you're trying to avoid now, would it?"

Screw this. I reach for the screwdriver again and he pulls it back. "Give it to me!" I demand.

"Not until you give me an answer." His smile taunts me. "Why aren't you showing up to class?"

"Because I don't like you." I narrow my eyes and try to use my frustration to sell the lie, because my problem is it's quite the contrary.

"Ehh," he says like a buzzer sound. "Try again."

"You're being childish."

"And you're not telling the truth."

I grit my teeth because what does he want me to tell him? That I think about him way too much when I'm not a woman who pines for a man? That I find myself wanting to walk next door to talk to him on the odd occasion that I see him outside? Odd occasion? Who am I fooling? I hear any noise from outside and I go to see if it's him. That I turned down a very viable hot night out with a guy because he wasn't him?

This is why I can't do this. *Why I can't do him.* I let my irritation with myself push me toward anger.

"Give me the screwdriver," I ask as I lunge at him, only to find myself flush against his chest, and his lips on mine.

I don't know who made the move, who I can blame later, but the kiss is instant and savage and laced with hunger and anger and every ounce of desperation I've felt over the past few days.

I take from him as much as he does from me. It's full of heat just as quickly as I realize I'm kissing him when I told myself I can't have him—that I can't set myself up for the devastation that comes with a guy like him. I push against his chest and tear my mouth from his.

I'm up on my feet in an instant, the word "Shit" a pant on my lips as I move as far away from him as I can in a space—*my space*—that seems completely consumed by him.

"Mind telling me why you're so mad at me?" His voice is right behind me—close, too close—and it's not enough that I smell his shampoo and soap and his taste is still on my tongue. He's owning my thoughts.

"Because I like you," I grit out. His laugh in response makes me clench my teeth tighter.

"I thought that would be a good thing, but I think I'm missing the whole estrogen-infused part of this conversation."

I hear his sarcasm and latch on to it, using it to fuel my anger when it's not his fault in the first place. "I don't want to like you."

His sigh is the only sound that accompanies the staccato of my heartbeat whooshing through my ears. "You're going to have to do better than that."

I whirl around and face him. His hips are leaning against my counter, his arms are folded across his chest, my dogs are sitting at his feet, and even though there is sarcasm tingeing every single word he says, there is patience in his eyes when I don't want there to be.

"Because this is how it happens for me, Reznor." I throw my hands up. "I start out not liking someone even though I think they're hot. Then I start to like them. I sleep with them a few times. I'm having fun. I'm not thinking about church bells—God, no. But then they say they want more. I say I don't want more. And in the blink of an eye, all the great sex we had turns awkward because regardless of what anyone says, monogamy is hard for people when it's casual. They expect to have to work for it. Working for it makes them feel like they deserve more out of it than incredible orgasms. And by then I'm exhausted, the fights become real, and every sign of affection is second-guessed to the point of mind-fucking it...and if I'm going to be fucking something, I sure as hell want some pleasure out of it." I suck in a huge breath when I finish rambling, only to find Reznor staring at me—eyes wide, brow narrowed, teeth sinking into his bottom lip to fight a smile.

"Jesus." He coughs the word out through a laugh. "And they say I'm the one who needs to go to therapy."

I should be offended, but I'm already on the defensive enough that his comment hits deaf ears. "You and me both, buddy," I mutter, wondering why I'm so heated about this. Why I'm fighting this.

It's because you really like him.

"Why?" he asks.

"Why what?"

"Just why? Why is this your position, and if it's your position, then why does it feel like you're digging your heels in to prove to yourself that it's valid?"

Everything about him right now calls to me. His patience. His calm demeanor when I just went off on him. The dark shadow the light casts over his face when I don't want to notice how gorgeous his eyes are or how sexy his lips look surrounded by the stubble he's let grow.

"Because nothing good ever lasts, that's why."

Chapter Fourteen

Reznor

Her words are soft but resolute when she says them, but the defeated look in her eyes betrays the conviction and defiance of her posture.

"I dis…" *I disagree*, I want to add but know she'll push back harder the other way to prove her point.

What is it, Desi, that makes you push me away when clearly you want me to stay?

At first I thought it had to do with the prowler—that she was closing herself off from men to protect herself and the vulnerability he'd made her feel—but it's so much more than that.

"Maybe you haven't found anything good enough that you're willing to work to make it last," I finally say.

Her eyes soften briefly—the door opening to reveal her thoughts—but as she realizes she was about to let me in, she turns her back to me and looks out the window. She stares at the silhouette of the hills beyond. They're dark against the setting sun's bright colors lighting up the sky. Pretty, but the woman standing with her hands on her hips and her head held high is much more attractive to me.

Attractive when I wasn't coming to Sunnyville to complicate my life, but damn it to hell, I like her kind of complication.

"Maybe I don't look at things that way," she explains. "Maybe I know I'm not the marrying kind and so why lead someone into thinking I am when in the end, they're just going to be pissed?"

"Why would they be pissed?" I ask but her back remains to me.

"Because it doesn't matter if you tell someone there will not be anything else, they still hope for more."

More. That damn word defines so much and not enough, and fuck if I'm not suddenly curious what *more* could be with a woman like Desi.

A woman like Desi?

How about, just Desi.

"Okay." I say the word, draw it out, and try to buy myself some time to figure out what the fuck is going on in my head. The same *what the fuck* that has me thinking about Desi more than I should when I know it goes well beyond being attracted to the *hard to get* vibe she gives off.

"I'm selfish with my time. I'm stubborn in my ways—hardheaded—and will fight you on it just to say I can. I love having fun. I love having great sex. But I also love my alone time and space too."

Music to my fucking ears.

I chuckle. Not because I'm making fun of her—which is what she must think given the expression on her face when she whirls around at the sound of it—but rather because I get it. *I get her.*

"You sound like me."

She stares at me, trying to figure out if she should believe me or not and for a split second, I think she does. But then I see the doubt creep in as her expression changes. "How? What do you mean?"

"I mean I have a job that requires me to be selfish. Every call could be my last. That doesn't exactly make me the stable, marrying kind either. I have to be able to breach a house and not worry that I could be leaving kids behind. That causes hesitation. That's a split second that could cost my team or me our lives…" I take a step toward her, hear her breath hitch when I reach out and tuck a loose piece of hair behind her ear. She shakes her head to avoid my touch. She's flustered. Cheeks are flushed. Pulse is racing in that spot beneath the angle of her jaw.

I want her right now.

"This can't happen," she murmurs, her chin lifting a smidge so her eyes can meet mine.

"I didn't ask for it to."

My fingers itch to touch her.

"But you were going to," she says.

My lips want to taste her.

"Reading my mind now, are you?"

My dick—it's already ten steps ahead of this conversation.

She takes a step back and I bite back my sigh of frustration. "This can't happen," she repeats. "The sex was too good. You're too…too everything, and it's a bad move."

Too everything? And that's a bad thing…why?

"Why?" If I'm going to be rejected, I might as well make her work for it since we both know she wants me as much as I want her right now.

"Because we'll ruin it. I'll get anxious and push you away. You're heading back to your real life at some point, so why should we do this?"

"Do what? Have sex you said was *too good?*"

"Yes. The first time."

"That's a good sign. Typically sex is never good the first time. It's usually miscommunication and worrying about whether the other person was satisfied. It's about learning the curves and the buttons and just what to do. You always want a second chance to show her you're much better than that...so if you think it was *too good* the first time, hell, Desi, just hold tight, sweetheart, because that means the second time is going to be mind-blowing." My smile is slow and deliberate when she looks my way. "One time with you is definitely not enough for me."

How you gonna handle that one, huh?

"Then it seems someone is going to have to figure out how to satisfy themselves somewhere else." She lifts a brow and folds her arms over her chest.

Looks as if someone just got their feet beneath them.

"You're the first woman who's told me I should sleep with someone else instead of them." I laugh and take a step toward her as she takes one back.

"That just goes to show I'm not like everyone else. I have my quirks. My flaws. My no-go zones." She puts a hand against my chest and pushes me back. "And you are a no-go zone."

"That's not what you said the other night."

We wage a visual war as the sexual tension thickens in the air between us.

"That was then, Reznor. This is now."

"What, without lust clouding your judgment?"

"Exactly."

"You'll want me back," I murmur as I move closer, and thank fuck for her obstinance because she doesn't move, which means her chest brushes ever so slightly against mine. But I see her body flinch—much like mine does.

"Nice try," she says quietly as she swallows the desire she's denying.

"Mmm." I lean in so my lips are so close to hers that we're breathing the same air. Her perfume fills my nose, and the shudder of her breath tells me I'm right. She wants me, she's just scared. "Late at night, when you're sliding your fingers between your thighs...you're not going to be satisfied with it. You're going to wish your fingers were me. You're going to want it to be me." I move my lips and murmur against her ear. "You'll come back."

I take a step back. She stands there frozen in place, nipples hard and pressing against her tank top, lips lax, and eyes heavy with desire. "Like hell I will," she says, but the conviction is lacking.

She knows it.

I know it.

"We'll see."

And with my dick screaming in protest, I nod and walk out the back door. *Fuck. This girl.* I've never had to fight this hard for someone, but somehow, I know this fight is worth something. *God, I want her...*She'll be back.

Let's hope I'm right.

Chapter Fifteen

Reznor

The gym was packed tonight.

Every single woman signed up for the class was there...all but one.

Damn it.

Where was she?

"Good class tonight, Reznor."

I look over to svelte Sandy and give her a subtle nod, the suggestion in her voice not fazing me in the least. "Thanks."

Her eyes give me a once-over as a slow smile spreads on her lips.

I ignore the open invitation and climb into the cab of my truck without another word.

A crazy man would turn that down...well, fuck if I'm not feeling crazy right now.

I dig my phone out of my center console where I locked it to see if she texted me.

Fucking nothing.

Shit.

I read the one from Grant: No update. No closer to finding who he was. I'll keep you updated.

I type off a quick thanks for the update he technically shouldn't be giving me about Desi's nameless, faceless suspect, rest my head on the seat and blow out a breath.

The woman is way more trouble than she's worth...but I still want her.

I startle when the phone rings and am even more surprised when I see Harry's name as the caller.

"Captain? What's up?" I ask, the smile on my face automatic.

"Just calling to check up on you and see how you're doing."

His words take me by surprise. Warning alarms sound off in my head. He's going to ask me to come back. Proceed with caution.

"I'm good. You?"

"Same ol' shit, different day." His chuckle fills the line. "That's good to hear. Has the time been good for you?"

"Yeah. I think so."

"That doesn't sound convincing."

"Nah. It's just...it's different."

"You miss it?"

I hesitate to respond and it shocks the hell out of me. "Parts of it. Yes."

"Bear said you're doing a killer job at the defense academy. He says women are lining up to be moved into your class...not like that fucking surprises me."

"Yeah, yeah, yeah." I laugh. "It's been a good change. Knowing that what I do might matter someday for someone."

"There's no adrenaline rush though, is there?"

Get to your point. I know it's coming.

"Nah." And he's right. There isn't. I'll give him that much. "But I needed the change of pace."

"The guys miss you," he says quietly, and the line falls silent as I figure out how to respond.

"I hear ya."

I miss them too. I do. But I also don't miss the constant pressure of having lives balancing on my decisions. Being here, I haven't felt that once.

"So you're coming back early, right?"

This time I give a half-hearted laugh. Took him long enough to ask it. "It's only been three weeks, Cap."

"Yeah, but Mars is in retrograde or some shit and all of the crazies are out."

"I think you mean Mercury."

"It could be marshmallows for all I care," he says, and I can hear the smile in his voice. "You're missed, Mayne. I know you've got three more weeks coming to you, but know what you contribute here. Experience, knowledge, leadership..."

"Thanks, Harry."

Before he ends the call I hear the laughing in the background, and that's when the pang of home hits me. The camaraderie.

I start the truck and put my arm on the windowsill, staring at the valley around me. The dark greens on the hills and terracotta-color buildings of downtown Sunnyville are nothing like the glass high-rises and steep hills of San Francisco. *My home.*

Then what the fuck am I doing here?

I shift into gear knowing damn well why this town has charm to me, and it has nothing to do with the town itself.

And everything to do with the brown-haired, blue-eyed, sassy woman living fifteen feet from me.

We may have only had sex one time, we may have sparred more than kissed...but sometimes, when you know someone might be worth the trouble, you know.

But well worth the trouble for what?

For me to want to stay? For me to want to have a fun-filled fling while I'm here? For me to pursue whatever this attraction is and see where it takes us?

My mind stutters over the answer. Not because I don't know it's true, but because I'm typically not one to think in these terms.

Terms that have intentional possibilities.

But I know.

The question is how do I make her see it too?

Chapter Sixteen

Desi

I shock awake—heart racing, pulse thumping, face beaded in sweat.

It takes me a second to orient myself to the fact that I'm in my room and not in Reznor's bed.

Because that was my dream.

Not a dark shadow standing over my bed. Not the paralyzing fear of what am I going to do.

Just the ache between my thighs of an orgasm denied.

I shove out of bed and walk to the kitchen to get some water, anything to clear the unsated desire owning my body so I *don't* march across the grass at two in the morning and break my own rules.

The dogs' collars jingle as they scratch and figure out if they want to raise their heads and watch what I'm doing or if they'd rather stay snuggled in their beds.

They choose beds.

Smart dogs.

I flick on the lights, grab a water from the fridge, and just as I turn mine off, I notice across the yard that Reznor's light is on.

Two damn peas in a pod.

Curiosity has me glancing his way.

His usually closed curtain that faces my direction is pulled back. He's facing me, the light at his back highlighting his silhouette, and the moonlight above casting enough light on his face that I can see his eyes. And *they* are looking right at me. His chest is bare, and I can't see anything below the sexy V of his hips, because just about at his hairline, the fence blocks my view.

He knows I'm here. He knows I'm watching him. He doesn't acknowledge me in any way, but I can feel him.

It makes no sense, and yet I can feel his awareness, his presence, and I can more than see the intense desire burning in his eyes when his hand slides over his stomach and below. I can't see his hand or his fingers, but I know they close around his shaft. It's in the bend of his elbow. The movement of his arm. The way his eyes close ever so slowly and his head falls back for the briefest of seconds.

I can't hear his groan but know he's emitting one. I can't hear the sound of his hand working over his cock, but I know he is.

And when he brings his head forward and locks his eyes on mine, teeth sinking into his bottom lip and his shoulders tense, my fingers find their way between my thighs.

It's my moan I hear now. It's my ache he's created that I'm trying to sate. It's him I'm thinking of as I slide my fingers down the seam of my sex until I find myself already wet, already wanting, already needing him.

My eyes close as I imagine it's Reznor's fingers in me. On me. Pleasuring me. And when I open them up, his eyes own mine. Like me, he's imagining the things he can't see.

His face is tense, his lips are lax, and everything about him oozes sex. But all I can do is remember his touch. All I can do is try to replicate it. All I can hope for is the same satisfaction.

But I'm as transfixed on him, on watching him come, as I am in bringing myself to climax, because there's something so intensely erotic and intimate in this unexpected moment. The mind-fucking. We can't hear each other, but we're forced to watch so we can see what we do to the other.

When he comes—head thrown back, arm jerking feverishly, the tendons in his neck taut with pleasure—I can all but feel the rumble of his groan and jerk of his hips as if he were standing between my thighs. And it's that thought, the one of me getting him off, that brings me to my own peak.

My breath grows harsher as my fingers move faster until the wall of pleasure slams into me.

And it does hit me...a soft wave of sensations I can sink into, but it's nothing like how Reznor made me feel. It is less intense. Shorter. Less pleasurable.

I'm far from sated.

But I show none of it to him as our eyes hold across the distance, because he was right.

I'm not satisfied.

Not in the least.

I still want *him*.

But when I move to pull my panties up, he's gone. His curtains are drawn, his light is off.

Goddamn you, Reznor Mayne.

This was never supposed to happen. Not you. Not me.

But God, how I want it to.

I want him.

Now.

Tomorrow.

That's all I'll allow myself to think about.

Because I don't deal in anything after that.

I can't.

I won't.

Then why is my mind wandering there?

Chapter Seventeen

Desi

Knock-knock. Knock-knock-knock.

"I don't want any," I yell over my shoulder as I bend to pick up Disco from where he's barking and wagging his tail in his kennel.

"I've heard that before," Reznor murmurs as he walks in the back door without being invited and rests a shoulder against the doorjamb.

It's much easier keeping my attention on Disco and the collar I'm putting around his neck than looking at Reznor.

We haven't talked since the other night. It's been a few days, and yet I fear if I look at him, defeat will be written over every part of my body. The kind of defeat that tells him he's right, I'm wrong, and oh yeah, can we have sex right now to make up for my stupidity?

"What do you want?" I ask without looking at him while I coo over Disco and head toward the front of the house. "Here you are," I say when I enter the main area of the grooming shop. Jeff is texting someone on his phone. He looks up when I enter, a smile wide on his lips when he sees Disco. I turn, surprised to see that Reznor stayed in the other room.

"Thanks. Ah, you look handsome as ever, Disc," Jeff says as he takes him from me.

"He was great per usual. That hot spot under his front arm looks better too."

"I thought it looked better so that's good to hear." Jeff hands a check to me, and I place it in my drawer. I half expect him to have one foot out the door when I turn back around, but he's standing there staring at me like he has more to say.

"What is it?" I ask.

"You're beautiful."

"Ah, that's sweet." But I'm suddenly uncomfortable. When Reznor said the same comment, I swooned. But with Jeff, there is no swooning. No nothing.

"I'm telling you, the offer still stands." A warm smile. "We were—"

"Good luck with that," Reznor's voice says from behind me, making both Jeff and me jump.

Jeff's smile fades as he takes in Reznor with his shoulder against the doorway, eyes burning a hole into him. Jeff gives Reznor the *fuck you* lift of his chin in greeting. "Hey."

Reznor doesn't say a word, but rather waits with a slight smirk—perhaps saying *fuck you* right back.

"Reznor, this is Officer Jeff Nelson—"

"Reznor Mayne," Reznor says, cutting me off and making his own introduction. "SFPD Swat Commander."

And the gauntlet has been thrown down, the pissing match commenced. But Reznor doesn't move from his spot against my wall, and Jeff stares at him for an uncomfortable space of time before he realizes *he's* the odd man out in this situation, when I'm more than certain he thought this whole interaction might go the other way. After all, Reznor is *in* my house and clearly isn't a client.

"Well, uh," Jeff says with a quick shake of his head before looking back at me, "thank you. Disco looks great as always. I'll uh...I'll talk to you later, Des."

I smile softly at him. "Talk to you later."

I wait for the door to shut behind him before I reprimand Reznor for his testosterone-laced claim that I never gave him the right to make.

"Really?" I ask, voice escalating as I turn and face him and his goading smirk.

"What did I do? I just told him good luck." He shrugs innocently. "He's gonna need it when it comes to you."

"Stop being an ass."

"An ass?" He takes a step toward me, body tense, posture telling me he'd welcome the fight I'm all too primed to give him. "You said I have no claim to you"—he throws his hands up as if he doesn't care—"so you've slept with him. I guess that means I need to go sleep with someone else to make it fair that—"

"No!" The word is out of my mouth before I can stop it. A simple knee-jerk reaction I wish I could take back, because I hate that I just gave him the upper hand.

His chuckle is low and grates on my ruffled nerves. "So there is something there then."

Gritting my teeth, I walk past him without responding. I find things that keep my hands busy—sweep the dog fur off the floor, dry the inside of the basin with a towel, realign the products on my shelf—all while he's standing behind me watching.

"I'll tell you what, Desi Whitman. I think you're a chicken. I think you hide behind your preconceived notions out of principle—or at least that's what you label it, but fear is fear. You can put lipstick on a pig, but it's still a pig." My hands still and my eyes meet his in the reflection of the window in front of me. "The question is, how bad do you want it? How bad do you want to see where this might go between us? A few nights of sex? A few dates? Anything. Something. When will you push yourself to think that it's okay?"

"I already told you, I know who I am, and I know what I want out of life."

"You did...but that's before you met someone who changed that."

I spin around and glare at him. He's thinking too much into this. "Down, boy. It's sex. One time. That's it."

"Two times," he counters and lifts his eyebrows.

"Two?"

"Sweetheart, we may not have been touching, but you can't deny we fucked each other across this space." He points to his house and back, but his eyes never leave mine. "You can call it semantics. You can say it didn't happen, but I'll fight you on that. Watching you was hotter than hell. You came for me. And next time you do, I'll be buried in you."

His words evoke too many things I don't want to think about but can't seem to avoid thinking of late.

"That's presumptuous," I say simply, because I have nothing else to say.

His chuckle is back and so is that look in his eye that's part challenge, part predator. "You're only pushing me away because you know it's good—we're good—and you're afraid you're only going to like it more."

"Why are you here, Reznor?" I shove my hands on my hips so I don't reach out and touch him.

I can see him question which answer he should give. The one we both know—that he wants to sleep with me again—or the underlying reason. "You didn't show up to class again."

"And I called Bear ahead of time and let him know that something came up. That way you knew, he knew—"

"Why not walk across the yard and tell me?"

"Because I was..." *avoiding you. Wanting you. Needing to keep my distance from you.*

His smile is half-cocked. "That's what I thought." He takes a step toward me. "You want me as much as I want you..."

"I don't—"

He holds his finger against my lips and says, "Shhh." Our eyes hold as every part of my body vibrates from his touch. "I'm not a patient man, Desi...except when it comes to things I think are worth it."

"Reznor—"

"Tell Jeff you're off the market." My spine stiffens at his order. "Because you're worth it."

And then, of course, the aftereffects of Reznor Maync hit me—the flutter, the swoon, and the sag—as a smile slides across his lips and he dips his chin before walking out the back door without looking back.

The man is infuriating.

Chapter Eighteen

Desi

Of course I show up to class.

The same gym. The same smell of sweat permeating the air. The same hot-ass instructor standing on the far side of the gym gently guiding women how to do what they need to do to defend themselves.

Then why do I suddenly feel completely defenseless when it comes to him?

Maybe for the same reason I've kept a low profile at the house for the past few days.

Because there's something about the man that makes me think about him when I shouldn't, want more of him when I should have already had my fill, and watch him do meaningless things outside his house when I have a ton of things to do myself.

Whew.

Get over there, Des. Quit standing and staring and wanting him when you keep telling yourself you don't.

"Ms. Whitman?"

Reznor's voice calling me from across the gym breaks through my thoughts and has me immediately on the defensive. I internally roll my eyes at him.

Our gazes meet briefly. "Glad to see you're here for today's class."

I snort—it's my only defense against that damn flutter his smile causes. "I was afraid if I didn't show that I might come home to my roof being re-shingled or something."

But damn...him in that snug shirt...his tight ass...and the smile he flashes my way. I swear he makes the women watching our interaction's panties wet....*so, yeah, he can re-shingle my roof any damn day.*

"I'll keep that in mind. Having a backup plan is always important." He steps toward the center of the mat and when I stand there, he lifts his eyebrows. "I require active participation, in case you forgot."

Oh, I didn't forget. *Don't bother giving me excuses. Just practice saying* yes.

"Coming," I mutter, but the deepening of his grin is all I need to know he heard me across the space—and exactly what I just said.

A couple of the women say hi to me as I step up to the edge of the mat and take a deep breath for Reznor-102.

"Shall we?" he asks before stepping over to me and grabbing my hand without another word.

"What?" I fight the knee jerk reaction to yank my arm back—the one that tells me his touch is too much to bear—when just last night I woke up with my hands between my thighs again, thoughts of him in my dreams.

"I've been missing my sparring partner," he says with a flash of a smile that to me says he wants to eat me alive.

Dear God.

Can everyone else see it? Or is it just me?

Because when Reznor uses me as a means to demonstrate to the rest of the ladies what to and what not to do, I have a hard time concentrating. His body is against mine—the heat of it, the feel of it, his cologne—and it's a tactile memory of when we had sex.

Every. Single. Time.

I know he knows it too.

"So let's run through another scenario," Reznor says, as he instructs me to lie down on the mat. "Let's say you're home alone, sound asleep in your bed." The hairs on the back of my neck stand up. "You wake up in the dark of night and there's someone standing over you." I clench my jaw and close my eyes momentarily as anger fires through my veins. *What the fuck?* "What would you do?"

Someone told him.

Not only did someone tell him, but rather than ask me about it to my face, he's confronting me here in front of strangers. Anger. Shame. Hurt. All three reverberate through me just like the question does: *Why would he do this?*

Maybe because if you're alone, he knows you'd dodge and avoid his questions like you have several times already.

"Desi?" Reznor asks, pulling me away from my thoughts and back to him. Seething is the best way to describe how I feel right now. "What would you do?" His eyes are kind when they look into mine, compassionate, and momentarily, I forget where we are and what is going on...and I want to talk to him about it.

And then I hear another class cheer over something, and the anger fires anew that he's using this as an example to prove a point to me. That he's exploiting my fear to make me pay attention to him.

"What would I do?" *I'd freeze like a coward and not defend myself.*

Heat stains my cheeks as I remember everything I didn't do to protect myself.

"Yes," he coaxes, clearly wary of my reaction.

"I—I don't know." My voice is barely a whisper as I confess my shortcomings. To him. To the class. To myself.

"That's okay," he says to the class, eyes still locked on mine. "That's why we're here—to learn what to do in this situation."

And so he teaches us different options of how to defend ourselves after waking up in the most vulnerable of states—groggy, disoriented, flat on your back, and at a stranger's complete mercy.

The entire time I try to engage, I try to do what he says, but my mind is so scattered. It's remembering how I cold I felt, how every beat of my heart sounded like thunder booming in my ears, how every hair on my body was raised in terror when I woke up seeing this hulking figure there. But now I also feel fury...Reznor knows what happened.

So what? Did he take it upon himself to find out? Did he call up Sunnyville PD or buy the guys some beers at Hooligan's Bar and ask them about quirky Desi Whitman who runs Doggy Style, *nudge-nudge wink-wink*, wouldn't you like to try that with her?

My stomach churns, and I'm already determined to call Grant and have him check out Reznor to make sure he's legitimate.

And then when class ends, as Reznor is high-fiving the ladies in the class and offering up praise, the thought hits me just as quickly as the panic that follows—what if Reznor and the man in my house were one and the same? What if I slept with...what if I really am that bad at judging a person and he is...

Oh my God. I have to get out of here.

My head spins as I rush to where my keys are. I run into a few women and mutter half-assed apologies, because I don't slow down and I don't want to.

I can't breathe.

New stranger in town who *coincidentally* moves next door to me a few weeks after a man was in my bedroom. A new stranger walks to my back door, not my front—when no one else does—and *coincidentally* that's how Grant thinks my creep gained access to my house.

Too many things. Too many thoughts. Too many—

"Desi."

My heart races as Reznor calls my name, but my feet don't stop as I rush out of the gym. I don't care about the scene I'm probably causing. I don't care who spreads what rumors about quirky Desi, because I'm used to them.

But I care about the panic attack that's owning every single part of me right now.

"Desi. Wait!"

I'm almost to my car when Reznor reaches for my bicep. The minute he touches me, I spin around. "Get your hands off me."

And there must be something in how I say it or on the look on my face, because Reznor takes a step back, his eyes narrowing as he stares at me.

"What's wrong?"

"Who are you?" I ask through gritted teeth, feeling like the crazy lady I probably sound like.

"*Des?* What's going on?"

"How did you know?"

He shakes his head and blinks, his expression one of utter confusion. "How did I know what?"

"About the man in my house? The scenario tonight. How did you know?" Tears threaten and although they don't show, the waver of my voice says otherwise.

I see the minute it clicks—what I'm accusing him of. His eyes widen and a part-laugh, part-what-the-fuck falls from his lips as he opens them and closes them and then opens them again. "You think...Wait a minute. You're serious, aren't you?"

The tears well as I question myself, my thoughts—everything. Now that he's standing in front of me, the picture of him standing over me like the other guy did isn't melding into the same one.

"I don't—I don't know what I think," I say, hating the confusion, the doubt, and the anxiety vibrating around inside me. He takes a step toward me, and I immediately retreat so my back is against the car, trapping me.

"Des, c'mon. I'm a cop for Christ's sake. I'm not—I could never..." I hate the look on his face, the one that reflects an adult coaxing a scared child out of hiding. *Me.* He stares, the muscle in his jaw pulsing, and then he's reaching for his phone in his pocket, pushes some buttons, and holds it out between us so the phone rings aloud, the speaker on. "Here. He'll tell you."

"Who?" I ask.

Ring.

"Grant Malone."

"Grant?" *What?* How does he know Grant?

Ring.

"Yes. He knows me."

"How? What—"

"Reznor Mayne. I knew you wouldn't be able to stay away from me for long." Grant's laugh comes through the line and every part of me that was primed for flight relaxes a little. "Did you have a come to Jesus and decide Sunnyville PD is where you want to be?"

"Yeah, yeah, yeah," Reznor says, his smile small and his eyes locked on mine as if he's daring me to not believe him.

"Spot's open. Ramos needs to fill it, and I told him I'm going to recruit your ugly ass."

"Nice try, Malone."

"Pussy."

"*Well.*" A half-laugh. "Hey, Grant, I have someone who needs you to vouch for me. That I am who I say I am."

"You getting yourself in trouble again?"

"Old habits might die hard, brother, but this is something a little different."

"What's up?" Grant asks as Reznor holds the phone out to me. "Rez?"

"Grant, it's me. Desi." My voice breaks with the words.

"Des? Is everything okay?" Concern floods Grant's voice.

"Yeah. Yes. I had a moment where…" I turn my back to Reznor as the tears flood my eyes and shame pushes them over the edge. "I'm fine. I was at self-defense and I had a flashback and I thought—I accused—I don't know what I thought."

"You thought Reznor was the perp?" There's surprise in his voice, but also understanding.

"I told you. My head's a mess, and I couldn't figure out how he knew—"

"I told Rez about what happened to you. He's a good guy, Des. He was probably trying to help you so you feel more settled about being able to take care of yourself."

"Mm-hmm." I don't trust myself to talk as the anxiety gives way to mortification. The anger to shame.

"He's one of the good ones. I promise."

"God, I'm an idiot." Until he responds, I'm not even sure I've said that out loud, but I sure as hell think it.

"No, you're not. We live in a safe community. When something like this happens it makes you question everything—yourself, what you thought was safe, everyone around you—and it's normal to have it rock you. I see it every day."

"Thanks."

"Hey, it wasn't that long ago. It'll get better. Then something will trigger the memory and it'll come back. Then it will get better again." He pauses and his voice softens. "Are you okay now?"

"Yes. Thanks. Sorry to bug you."

The call ends, and I stand with my head hanging forward, my back to Reznor, and hate everything in this moment but him. I attempt to collect myself but know it's no use.

I just made a complete ass out of myself.

"Look, I'm sorry," I say as I turn around and hand him his phone, but refuse to meet his eyes. "I...you took me by surprise and then my mind started running with it and—no excuses, I fucked up."

"Hey. Shh," he murmurs as he reaches out and lifts my chin so I'm forced to look at him.

But the smug expression I expected to see is nowhere in sight. The sarcastic response I thought would be next is non-existent. I'm met with a soft smile and compassion flooding through those brown eyes of his.

And all I want to do is step into his arms and let him comfort me.

But that's a scary thought for me. Needing him. Wanting to need him.

"Look, I'm sorry, Des. I didn't mean to—"

"I don't need to be coddled. I'm fine. He's gone—whoever he is, and so the whole thing is over with." I roll my eyes and try to add more conviction to my words than I really feel. "I only took the class to get Grant off my back."

"Uh-huh," he says with a look that tells me he's not buying what I'm selling. "And your assumption that I was your perp had nothing to do with being scared of your own shadow."

"Sorry." I shake my head from his touch, and step back trying to collect my thoughts. "I need to go home. I just need..."

To trust my own judgment? To not accuse others because I'm

paranoid? To settle back into my quirky world that seems to have fallen to the wayside since that night? *Alone.*

"Don't go home," he murmurs.

"It's probably for the best."

We stand in the waning light of the fall evening, cars coming and going out of the high school parking lot, and stare at each other, uncertainty about what's going on here more than paramount between us.

"I want to take you somewhere."

"Reznor—"

"Just trust me."

"I don't think—"

"That's the problem, isn't it? Thinking?" he asks with a wink and a convincing smile. "I'm not taking no for an answer."

Ah yes, I forgot...I have to practice saying yes.

Chapter Nineteen

Desi

"What the heck?" I say through a laugh as we pull into the empty lot in Melville—the next town over. The area has been transformed with a makeshift structure taking up the most of it. Black Visqueen lines the exterior walls with caution tape as its accent. A strobe light can be seen at the entrance, as can a person dressed in a clown costume taking tickets of mostly high school-aged kids. "Reznor?" I ask as he pulls into a parking spot.

"Trust me."

I don't even get a chance to respond before he's out of his truck and circling the hood to open the door for me.

"A haunted house?"

"Just trust me."

I eye him, finding this completely bizarre, but I'm away from my house and it's definitely something to distract me from the embarrassment of earlier. "C'mon, Desi Whitman. You know you're curious about why I took you to a haunted house out of the blue."

He looks adorable—the playful look in his eye, the off-kilter smile, the hand he has extended to me—and I know I won't resist him.

"Are you hoping that I get scared and jump into your arms?" I ask as I take his hand and exit the truck. "Because if that's the case, you're no better than Jared Ingram, who dared me to go to one in ninth grade so he could try and make out with me."

"Was he successful?" Reznor asks. The funny thing is, when he pulls his hand from mine as we fall into step next to each other, a part of me sags inside. The part that is rebelling against my typical policy of no contact, no semblance of dating, nothing romance-y...because who likes that gooey shit anyway?

But I sag.

Shit. First flutters. Then swooning. And now sagging.

"Des?"

"Oh. Sorry. I was thinking about sagging."

"What?" He barks out a laugh and mine isn't far behind. "Sagging? Do I even want to know?"

"It's—never mind." I wave a hand. What else can I do tonight to make a fool of myself? But I am laughing. He's making me laugh. That's always a good sign. "Jared Ingram. Man, he tried, but the boy was a terrible kisser."

"Nothing worse than that," he says, placing a hand on my lower back as we step into the line to buy tickets.

"It's the kiss of death," I joke.

"Good thing you're here with me. That's a sign I'm not going to die the fate of poor Jared." Reznor flashes a killer smile at me and winks before stepping up to the booth to buy our tickets.

The scent of kettle corn fills the air and the chatter of teenagers and their laughter echoes in the air around us. Muted screams of fright can be heard from the depths of the open-doored haunted house. People mill about in groups with caramel apples in hand.

But my attention turns to Reznor. To his easy charm with the woman selling tickets. To the sincerity in his smile. To the strong lines of his profile.

What are you doing here, Des? This looks like a date. It feels like a date.

But I know.

I don't want to admit it to myself, but the man has my attention in more ways than one.

"What?" he asks when he catches me staring at him.

"I'm curious why we're here."

"You'll find out soon enough," he says cryptically as the person running the haunted house lets the next group of people enter. "We're next."

I take a deep breath and anticipation begins to stir to life in my veins as the group that just entered screams at something inside. I'm not a scaredy-cat by any means, but haunted houses aren't exactly something I'd choose to go do on my own.

Don't be a chicken.

The attendant motions for us to step forward and enter as my heart begins to pound in my chest.

"Our turn," Reznor murmurs. He places a hand on the small of my back to usher me forward, but it does nothing to ease the sudden fear of what waits for us in the pitch-dark beyond the first corner.

"Uh-oh, you go first," I say as I step behind him and grip his shirt on either side of his torso.

The first room is an eerie graveyard. Tombstones, body parts sticking out of dirt, and a low layer of smoke set the stage for us as my eyes flicker everywhere and anywhere to try and see what or who will jump out at us.

We make it through the room, but the minute we hit the next one full of strobe lights and zombies frozen in place, I know I should have peed before we did this.

As we reach the middle of the room, a zombie—that looks like he is plastic—jumps to life and scares the shit out of us. Then and only then that I get a clue what we are doing here.

Reznor's screech at the top of his lungs when the character lunges at us is deafening. His body is fraught with tension, and he takes me by total surprise when he pushes me ahead of him and buries his forehead against my shoulder to hide his eyes.

"Walk, Des. Just please fucking walk," he orders as his hands shake and his body pushes against mine to go faster.

My own adrenaline is charging through me, so I don't question why he is throwing me into the fire when he's supposed to be the tough guy. But with each and every room we enter, his reaction is so extreme I can't help but laugh at some of them. Jumping behind me. Screaming at the character to get the fuck away from him. The grip of his hands on my body. The command in his voice as he tells me what to do.

And just when I think the poor guy is going to have a heart attack, we push into the last room to find that we have successfully made it through the haunted house.

"Jesus fucking Christ," he swears harshly as he all but jogs as far as he can from the exit, hands behind his head, feet moving one way and then the other as he tries to shake off the rush of fear that's coursing through him.

As I stand to the side and give him the space he needs, I wonder what the point of this whole exercise was. And what it is he's trying to tell me with it.

He blows out a huge breath and looks back at me—there's a line of sweat on his brow and his face is pale.

"You okay?" I ask.

"I'll be fine. In a few minutes." A pace one way, then the other. "I hate those fucking things."

This time when he strides toward me, he grabs my hand without asking, forcing me to follow him.

"What—?"

"I'm hungry."

"Whoa—okay."

He's silent as he proceeds to buy what appears to be one of each item from the concession stand, much to the teenage girl's chagrin who is making googly eyes at him as she waits on him. It's not until we're seated at a picnic table on the far end of the lot, where the light is dim and the crowd is sparse, that he finally looks at me.

"Have you figured it out yet?" he asks as he takes a bite of nachos.

"Yes, but…"

"But what? I'm a big, bad cop who most days deals with monsters for a living, but put me in a haunted house and I scream like a little girl?"

I laugh and take a chip of my own. "Something like that."

He smiles and then it fades as his eyes grow serious. "We all have fears, Desi. Even the strongest of us have fears. It's okay to have one—or many. It doesn't make you weaker…it makes you human."

His words hit home. The compassion in his voice more so as I open my mouth to respond and then shut it, fearful that the tears burning in my eyes will fall.

"Do you know what it's like to feel like you're one hundred percent vulnerable? To wake up in your own bed and know you are at the complete mercy of someone else? Then the utter terror of that person leaving and knowing they are still out there, and might possibly still come back? The jumping at every shadow and being suspicious of every new person you meet who seems overly friendly? And more than anything, questioning yourself: your judgment, whether you brought this on yourself…and how you reacted nowhere near how you thought you would in that situation?" The words fall out in a rush as thoughts, feelings, doubts I've had for weeks finally materialize.

"Feels good to finally say it, doesn't it?" he asks with his head angled to the side and a finger tracing lightly over the top of my hand.

I avert my eyes, suddenly shy, even though I'm never shy, and allow the smile to slide on my lips. "Yeah, it does."

The carnival-like atmosphere carries on around us but for the moment, it just feels like it's him and me—no one else matters.

And there go the flutters again.

Crap.

"It's normal, you know," he says.

"Not for me, it isn't," I respond, referring to the aftereffects of the prowler and the damn fluttering.

"Let me guess—tough girl, life of the party who loves the limelight and has no problem being the one who makes people at ease, the one everyone depends on when things go to shit."

I laugh, surprised by how much he has me pegged. "Always the bridesmaid, never the bride."

He falls quiet for a moment but his eyes question and ponder something for a beat. "I thought you were okay with that."

"God, yes," I say with a little more enthusiasm than I should. "That sounded bad. I just mean—dogs are more loyal than most men."

"So instead of the crazy cat lady named Jana who lives in the corner house, you're the dedicated dog lady who lives in the yellow clapboard."

"Pretty much." I laugh. "And perfectly fine with it."

"You might change your opinion someday," he says, and I swear to God that look in his eyes right now, the one that's part amused, part serious—but *wholly* invested in every single response I give—could very well make me change my answer.

The thought stuns me. Unnerves me. Makes me panic because I don't think that way.

"So when are you heading back to San Francisco?" I ask the question because I need to remind myself he'll be gone soon. That I can't fall prey to the flutters and the swoons because he will be gone soon and that's...*that's exactly how I like it.*

But my mind stutters over those six words. Over my normal response that now doesn't feel so normal. *Because that's exactly how I've liked it.*

His eyes hold mine, the flash of surprise at my sudden change of topic there, but I appreciate that he doesn't call me on it. He nods his head in silent acceptance. It's as if he knows the question can't be avoided. It's valid, and truly, he doesn't have any right to call me out on my fears when he can't offer me anything. *And somehow, that stings.*

"Three weeks. Four. It could be sooner unless I find something here that piques my interest enough to want to stay."

Three weeks. Twenty-one days. Unless something piques his interest. Not someone. So why is he here with me? Why push for something so temporary? Because he's horny? Because I'm convenient?

Jesus, Des. Aren't you the first person to push someone away? Aren't you the one putting the brakes on things with a man? So why does this bug you? Why does his blasé response sting? I feel emotionally exhausted and spent, yet not ready to return home either.

And so we sit in this awkward state where I'm hurt but shouldn't be and he doesn't realize it. He takes a sip from his Slurpee and we turn to watch a group of teens to the left, re-enacting their reactions to their experience in the haunted house. "Do you have any family around here?"

I look back at him but he's still watching the kids. "Nah. My mom lives in Idaho."

"And your dad?"

"Don't know." I shrug. "He left when I was one, and after that my mom always had a boyfriend for a few months on, few months off...and on and on. A constant cycle of someone moving in, getting used to a new person in our house, and then just as we settled down into a routine, they'd break up. The revolving relationship door isn't for me."

"Who said it has to be that way?"

I twist my lips as I try to put my thoughts to words. "Right or wrong, I think I conditioned myself to have fun, and when the fun starts to become something more, I shift gears and move on. I'm good with dating. With enjoying the moment. The future's going to happen whether I worry about it or not, so why even bother?"

Reznor's eyes are intense when he stares into mine. "Makes sense. I can respect that." There is no judgment in his tone, and there's something about him that makes me feel comfortable being me—makes me feel comfortable telling the truth—when most of the time I say what I need to say to play the role society feels I should. "What about you? Why aren't you married to Mrs. Stepford?" I ask. "Don't think the spotlight you're shining on me isn't going to turn toward you and ask the same question."

But why am I asking? Do I really want to know his answer or am I just trying to get out from under the microscope that will magnify my hidden cracks and atypical shortcomings?

He takes a sip as his smile falls quiet and his eyes meet mine. "First off, Stepford is far from my type."

"What is your type then?"

"Long-legged brunettes who love to wear bold colors, smell like wet dogs, and have a wicked kiss."

I hate that with every word my body reacts more to him. The ache between my thighs. The flutter in my belly. The swooning in my mind.

"That was smooth," I say to try and distract myself.

"You like that?" He lifts an eyebrow. "I was going to add who likes to groom Pussy, but thought that might be a bit crass."

I throw my head back and laugh and think of that damn cat and love and hate her all simultaneously for getting us to meet each other.

"Well...it is groomed."

What are you doing?

"Is that so?" he asks with a slight smile and a darkening of his eyes.

You swore off him.

"Yep."

One more time can't hurt that much, can it?

"I think you need to take me home and see for yourself."

Reznor stands abruptly from the table, hand on my elbow, feet leading the way. "I thought you'd never ask," he murmurs.

Chapter Twenty

Reznor

The car ride is silent.

Every attempt at conversation falls flat almost as if we're afraid an extra word might spark the sexual tension eating up the air in the car.

I pull into the driveway without even giving a thought to the fact that her car is still at the high school. We'll get it tomorrow.

Right now I plan on following through with my *the second time it's way better* line. And no, the getting off watching her get off didn't really count as a second time.

Because fuck if I haven't thought about doing this with her since she left my bedroom the last time.

Yeah, I have a problem. A big one. And her name is Desi Whitman.

Our feet clomp up the stairs of her porch. My eyes are on her hips, her ass, thinking about those long legs being wrapped around me as she fumbles with the key in her lock.

I like that she's nervous.

It means she cares.

It means she wants this as fucking badly as I do.

The minute the door opens and I shut it behind us, it's like dynamite detonates. We're on each other in an instant. Hands and lips and tongues and bodies grinding against each other as we strip off our clothes in a mad dash to see who can get undressed quicker.

Her shirt is over her head. My lips are on her neck. Her back bumps against the wall behind her. A laugh falls from our mouths seconds before my lips close over the soft peak of her nipple, making both of us moan and slow for a beat.

Dogs bark somewhere in the house.

There is no slow. There's only desperation and greed and every pleasurably selfish sensation in between. It may have been only two weeks since the last time we had sex, but right now it feels like for-fucking-ever.

Her hands are on my pants, shoving them down so my dick can spring free. Hurried whispers. Desperate groans. Another wall but this time at my back.

Laughter murmured by lips pressed against skin.

The jingle of collars down the hall as a dog shakes his head.

My hand slides between her thighs to feel her wet just before she drops to her knees. With those big eyes of her angled up to mine, she wraps her lips around my cock, and I watch every damn inch of it disappear into that sexy mouth of hers.

Fucking Christ Almighty. The woman doesn't have a gag reflex.

My cock sits at the back of her throat as her fingernails scratch ever so slightly the skin beneath my balls. She suctions tight around me and slowly slides it back out so it releases from her mouth with a popping sound. Her tongue circles around my crest, dips into the split at the end and the moan she makes—the one that tells me she likes how I taste—is enough to make me want to come right there and show her how much she'd enjoy it.

And so I face the worst dilemma known to a man. Let her suck me off with that all-powerful suction of her lips, or bury myself in her hot, wet, and tight pussy so I can prolong the pleasure and get her off in the process.

She swallows me again, my dick going as far as it can before she wraps her fingers around what's exposed and begins working that angle too.

Sweet. Fucking. Heaven.

For a moment I let myself get lost in the sensation. My head falls back. My hand fists in her hair to help her mouth fuck me. My hips thrust forward with each bob forward of her head.

And when I know I'm almost to the point of no return, I step back abruptly and lift her off the floor. She squeals as I haul her naked ass over my shoulder and with a resolute slap to it say, "Tell me which room, sweets, or you're going to end up getting nailed against this wall right here."

"Yes. Please." Her hands slide down my back and cup my ass as the scent of her pussy so close to my face is like a fix to a junkie. It owns my thoughts. "Let's start with the wall, and move to the bed for round two."

I let her body slide down my shoulder until her legs are wrapped around my hips and her back is resting against the wall. Her eyes are on mine—I barely see them in the moonlit room, but I feel the heat of her pussy against my waist.

"I like the way you think."

"And I like the way you fuck," she says seconds before I lift her hips up and push my dick into her.

Every inch of my body vibrates from wanting to come instantaneously, at how incredible she feels wrapped around my cock. Every. Single. Inch.

Her lips slant over mine and she takes control as she slides her tongue between my lips to urge me to move.

And I do.

* * *

Her room suits her. It's bright and eccentric and a little bit of everything thrown all together, but it works.

At least that's what it looks like from where I'm sitting, propped on a shit ton of pillows against her headboard, staring at her.

"Why don't you come back here and lie down?"

Her hand freezes midway to whatever she was reaching for. *Yes, Desi, that means I'm not leaving here. That means I'm not done with you yet. Not by a long stretch.*

She turns and looks at me from where she stands looking out the window to the darkness beyond. She's still naked, her hair a mess, but I can tell she's already trying to figure out her next move, when that next move is going to be coming back to bed with me.

It takes her a beat and for me to pat the bed, but she slowly makes her way and slides in beside me. I feel her stiffen when I pull her close to me so her head is against my shoulder and my arm is wrapped around her back.

We sit in an awkward silence as she tries to come to terms with what this cuddling thing is. It's almost comical how I can feel her tense every time I shift a millimeter as if she's afraid to touch me, when minutes ago I was buried balls deep in her.

But slowly she relaxes, and her fingers begin to draw aimlessly on my arm.

"What are your tattoos of?" It's the first time she's spoken, and it doesn't surprise me that it's to shift the focus elsewhere.

Everyone has a story to tell...they are my story. I sigh. My mantra. But this is Desi...and for some reason I want to talk when I normally don't. For some reason, I feel compelled to tell her my story. "When I was younger, I was a real piece of work. I was out of control. Always in trouble."

"And you're a cop?" She laughs.

"It was the only thing that saved me. I was walking that fine line—could have gone either way, convict or cop—and I chose cop."

"Do you mind me asking what happened?"

I lick my lips and trace my finger up and down the line of her spine. "Rough upbringing. My dad thought fists were the best form of fear, but what he didn't understand was that it made me crave that form of attention. Eventually, I didn't fear the bad, just the good." I chuckle at the thought. At the memory of the sound of his voice when he'd call me "Sonny boy" and how those two words meant I was about to get my ass kicked. "I started doing petty shit. Stealing this or that. Vandalism. I fell into the wrong crowd as you'd expect, and one night I went on a ride with them, not knowing what they knew. They'd brought guns along. Held up a convenience store and the minute the shots were fired, they ran to flee while I stood there staring at the blood seeping from the clerk's chest."

"Jesus, Rez."

"Yeah, well...they left without asking me to go. Thought they'd leave me there to take the fall for them since I was clearly on the CCV television the store had. I stayed all right, but I also called 9-1-1 and applied pressure to the wound to help stop the bleeding." I can still remember the taste of fear in my mouth. Watching his blood stain between my fingers as I pressed against the wound with my T-shirt. "Obviously I didn't cover for the kids but pointed them out. That put a target on my back so...I left. Moved a few cities north to one where I could get lost in its population, and joined the Academy."

"That's crazy," she says. And she doesn't even know the half of it.

"What about you? Why the dog grooming business?"

She snorts. "Because dogs are way more loyal than men."

Ah, we're back to that here?

"Is that so?" I take advantage of her head tilted to look at me and press my lips against hers. I kiss her gently, my tongue slipping between her lips and teasing her without any sense of urgency. Her body softens as I worship her mouth in a kiss that I can feel all the way to the bottom of my balls.

Jesus.

The woman knows how to knock a man on his ass.

And just as quietly as we slipped into this kiss, Desi pushes away from me and sits up. The draw of her breath is shaky and the way her hands play with the quilt on the bed, anxious.

I study her. Fear is rolling off her. "You just can't do it, can you?" I ask into the darkness of the room.

"Do what?"

"Let your guard down for one second."

"That's crap," she says through a laugh, but I can hear the truth edging her words.

"You change the subject every time I ask about more of you. You push away every time the kiss becomes too serious. You—"

"I don't do that," she asserts, but she damn well knows she does.

"Then why is it so hard for you to lie here in bed with me and just...and just be."

"Because beds are for sleeping or for sex."

"Then come here, let's go to sleep." I reach out to pull her toward me to call her bluff, and when she swats my hands away, I know it worked.

"No."

"Why not?"

"Because it's...it's too close."

"It's too close?" I laugh. "I can stick my dick in you, but lying beside me is too close to you?"

"It's not the same." She huffs.

"You're right. It's not. And the having sex part is the one that makes us closer than sharing the same sheets if I'm not mistaken." I run my hand down her back in an attempt to show her I can touch her and it's okay. "Why do I make you uncomfortable?"

"You don't."

My chuckle is the only sound in the room. "I'm a negotiator, Desi. Trained to listen to what's not being said and see things that others are trying to hide...so, nice try."

"God, you're a pain in the ass," she groans.

"And you're a confusing one."

"Actually quite the contrary," she says as she turns to face me and sits cross-legged. Her perfect tits are on display and the dark patch of hair covering her pussy blends in with the shadows and makes me want to play hide-and-go-seek to find it.

But her eyes watch mine as I scrape them up every inch of her naked flesh until they meet her gaze again.

"Where were we?" I laugh.

"We were talking about how I'm not confusing but rather am every guy's dream."

"Every guy's? I was hoping just mine," I murmur as my finger traces up the inside of her thigh so she squirms when I slide it ever so softly over those lips of hers, still swollen from our first round.

"That's the problem."

"What?" I ask, distracted by the slickness I find there.

"The problem is you."

"Me?" She moans as I slip my finger between them and coat it with her arousal. "What did I do besides give you an incredible orgasm?"

Her smile is seductive, as is knowing how wet I make her. Her nipples pebble and her head falls back as I slip my finger into her.

Christ. This woman. She's so careful, so guarded, yet there's something about her—something that's untouched—that I want to get to know. It's not just that she's vulnerable, but she's also fucking strong. *And I like that.* After what she said about her mom, it makes sense why she doesn't believe men are capable of sticking around. Shit, until I met her, I was the same. I'm not a man who falls for a woman, but hell if she's not tripping up my feet so I do.

"I affect you," I murmur.

"So…" she moans and tightens around me.

"So why are you mad at me for that?" I ask as I curve my finger to rub against her G-spot as my other hand runs up and down the length of my shaft.

She widens her legs to give me better access and leans back on her hands. "This is the last time, Reznor. No more after this. I mean it."

I smile.

Sure thing, Des.

Until next time.

Chapter Twenty-One

Desi

"Come on, you little heathen."

Matilda wiggles and shakes and suds fly all over the place, causing me to look up and then still when I see Reznor across the way. His shirt is off and he's bent over looking at something on his front porch, biceps flexed, ass perfectly positioned, and I simply stand and watch him.

Distracted.

Mesmerized.

Recalling how deliciously fine he was the other night. *And morning.*

Break the habit, Des.

Wasn't that what I swore to myself when he walked out? That I was going to break the habit he'd created in me wanting him?

But here's what I don't know. Do I break the habit so I stick to my guns about only needing casual sex, or is it so I don't get hurt when he moves away?

I know the answer, but I don't think I'm ready to admit it to myself yet.

I like that he doesn't push me. Yeah, he kind of does, but in a cute, *come on, let's have incredible sex* kind of way.

I like that when he's not with me, I kind of miss him.

I like that—*Shit.*

"Knock it off, Des," I mutter. "I can't let myself do this, Matilda. I just can't. There I go again talking to myself about the reasons why I can justify sleeping with him." I look back up at Reznor and shake my head. "But wouldn't you sleep with him if he looked like that?" I ask the sodden mutt.

Yep. I've lost my mind.

But that's the problem. I think about him way too much. Like the kind of thinking about him where I have little daydreams imagining what it would be like if he weren't going back to San Francisco in the coming weeks.

It's just sex. It's just sexy Reznor. That's all it is.

Then why am I standing here with a soaking wet dog and staring at him and not tending to her?

Because he makes me wet too.

Matilda shakes again and water sprays on me. "Yeah, yeah, yeah," I say to her. "Good thing you're so cute or else I'd be mad at you for that."

I busy myself rinsing the suds from her and then towel dry her because Em's putting Taylor down. I love that kid to death, but she's a holy terror if she doesn't get her nap. And nap time means I get alone time with my best friend—something that's few and far between these days.

The clomping on the front porch immediately has my attention as I bolt for the front door to answer it before the doorbell rings.

I fling the door open and of course, it's Reznor, standing there with his shirt off and that cocky smirk on his face.

"Don't ring it!"

"Ring what?" he says, confusion etched on his face.

"The bell."

He laughs. "I do believe I've already rung your bell a time or two."

Every part of me thanks God that Emerson is not standing in the room behind me hearing this or witnessing the look in Reznor's eyes that tells me he'd be game to go right now if I said it was okay.

"Aren't you proud of me?" he asks.

"For what?"

"I came to the front door." He flashes a lightning-quick grin.

"Good boy."

"Don't I get a treat?" he asks with a lift of his brow and eyes that run the entire length of my body in slow appreciation before stepping past me into my living room uninvited.

And I'd be lying if I said that slight brush of his body against mine doesn't do things to every part of me.

"Can I help you?" I manage when I notice he has an electric drill in one hand and a large bag of something in his other.

"I'm not sure if you want me to answer that," he says, followed by a low rumbling chuckle as he sets his stuff on the coffee table and turns toward me.

Damn the man gives good face.

Our eyes hold across the small space, and every part of my body is more than aware of him, his cologne, the look in his eyes...just everything. *And* including how much I wish Emerson wasn't here right now so I could scratch this itch that seems to keep coming back somehow.

You promised, Des. No more sex with him.

"Is it Pussy again? Is she wet?" he asks, a ghost of a smile turning up the corners of his mouth. I'd swear he rehearsed the timing, because just as the words are out of his mouth, Emerson enters the room, mouth wide, cheeks flushed.

"I'm sorry, I didn't realize I was...I'll just"—she looks back and forth between us then throws a thumb over her shoulder—"go back in here, and you can pretend I'm not here."

"No. Em. You're fine." I glare at Reznor. "He's talking about Logan's cat, Pussy." Emerson eyes me. "I'm serious. The first time we met—it was—it's just a joke between us. Reznor Mayne, please meet my best friend, Emerson Malone. Em, this is my new, temporary neighbor, Reznor."

"Oh my God. Yes. Grant was telling me about your Academy days last week." She crosses the small space, tucking her strawberry-blonde hair behind her ear before reaching her hand out to shake his. "So nice to meet you."

"Likewise." They shake. "Is it really true you own a skydiving company?"

"That it is. At Miner's Airfield. It's called Wings Out."

"I might have to take a trip out there and have a jump while I'm here."

"Please do," she says and just my luck the two of them would get on perfectly. They continue talking for a few minutes to the point that I'm curious if I snuck out of the room if they'd even notice.

And then, almost as if I can physically see the light bulb turn on in Emerson's head—when it hits her that there just might be more here than meets the eye—she gasps out, "Oh. I'm sorry. I'm just...I think I hear Taylor crying. I'll go check on her." She hooks a thumb over her shoulder but doesn't move, a sly, knowing smile ghosting her lips.

"It's okay," Reznor says. "I didn't mean to interrupt." He holds up the stuff in his hands. "I should've called, but I bought you an infrared security system. Nothing extensive, but enough to alert you if the doors or windows are opened. I can come back and install it another time."

"No," Emerson gasps. And that one word expresses perfectly how what he just said makes me feel. It's a good thing she speaks, because right now I'm pretty speechless as I stare at him, dumbfounded.

He bought me an alarm system. He came to the front door. He's trying to take away the fear.

"I can come back. I didn't know there was a baby—"

"She sleeps through anything," Emerson says with a wave of her hand and I can already see Reznor winning her over.

"I'll be as quiet as possible."

"Don't worry about it. She'll love more time with Aunty Des. Please, do your thing...Des and I can visit out back so we're out of your way."

Reznor looks at me and gives me a shy smile with a lift of his eyebrows, a silent request for permission, and it takes me a second to find my voice. "Thank you." We hold each other's gazes for a beat longer before I look up to see Emerson fighting a smile and pointing to me that we need to talk.

Because I've been holding out on her.

* * *

"He bought you an alarm system."

"So?" I play it off, although that in itself is a flutter, swoon, and sag all in one.

"That's like oral sex times one thousand."

"Shh. Quiet down, you horny pregnant woman." I laugh.

She leans back in her chair, hands folded over her swollen belly, and stares at me. "So, are you going to elaborate on what is going on here between you and Mr. Sex on a Stick in there? Does he sex you so good you say blah-blah-blah?"

"Who said...we haven't...it's just—"

"Sounds like someone's saying blah-blah-blah"—she laughs—"so I'll put a checkmark in the incredible-sex box, thank you very much."

"He's just...infuriating. And does everything just right. And he—gah—he doesn't back down—and, never mind. It's hard to explain."

Her laugh is full and her belly moves with it. "Those are the best kind of men, sweetheart." And of course, she would know, given her husband. She's clearly amused by my inability to talk coherently. "The ones who you can't describe and can't stop thinking about."

"Whatever. You know me, I don't get like that with guys."

"Uh-huh," she says with a lift of her brows and a knowing smile.

"Seriously. He's just nice, and it's been a while since I've met a decent and nice guy—"

"Who's incredible in bed. Comes over and fixes your broken pipes—

"

"How did you—?"

She holds up her hand to cut me off. "Grant told me," she says, throwing me for a loop.

"Wait, you knew about him and didn't tell me?"

"Ha. Don't get your feelings hurt, sister, because it's not like you told me about him either." She holds her finger up to stop me when I begin to talk. "I'm not finished with my list yet."

"You and your lists."

"Where was I? Oh. Right. Who's teaching you self-defense. Who's installing an alarm system. Who has you stuttering out a response." She eyes me. "Should I continue?"

Our eyes meet, hold, and then I lower mine to look at my hands folded and fidgeting on the table. "It's complicated," I murmur as Reznor walks past the window, phone to his ear, the tenor of his laugh soft so as to not wake up Taylor but still vibrating to where we're sitting.

"He fits in seamlessly," she says. "Even the dogs don't get worked up over him like they do everyone else."

I nod and stare at him through the window as the drill sounds off and he reaches above his head to install an infrared monitor.

How was it that two months ago I didn't even know him? It's almost as if I can't remember not having him here or nearby...and that's scary. *He fits in seamlessly.*

"You're in love with him, aren't you?"

I sputter and then choke on a breath as I rip my eyes from him and look at her wide-eyed and in disbelief. "Will you shut up?" I gasp. "You're being utterly ridiculous."

A smile curls up one side of her lips. "You never answered my question. Are you?"

"How can you even ask me that?" I glance to where Reznor was to make sure he's still there and out of earshot of this asinine conversation. "I've known him less than two months."

Memories of growing up flicker in my mind: a new man would start coming around, a new declaration of love by my mother shortly thereafter, a swift departure by said man within weeks.

That's not me. *I'm not her.*

"Two months...meh." Emerson shrugs. "I know people who have fallen in love in a lot less time."

"We are *not* having this conversation right now."

"Why not? Does it make you uncomfortable?" I hate the *cat ate the canary* grin and how her words are making my mind spin and question and wonder.

"You need to be quiet. He's not...I don't...this is just—"

"All I'm hearing is blah-blah-blah," she teases, and after all the shit I gave her—pushed on her when she was dating Grant—I know she's enjoying the hell out of this.

"I'm not in love with him," I assert in a harsh whisper so she takes me seriously, *and* so Reznor doesn't hear me.

"But you're in a whole lotta like with him."

"What's not to like? He's hotter than hell and good in bed."

"I think he's a whole lot more than hot to you. That you neglected to tell me you were hooking up with him speaks for itself."

"Slow down, turbo. It's only been a few times."

"Exactly." She lifts her eyebrows. "Only a few times when he lives twenty feet away means you guys don't want to ruin this so you are trying to take it slow. I can respect that."

"Earth to Emerson? Are you listening to yourself? This is me we're talking about here." I laugh, but it's solely to abate the nerves this conversation is giving me. If she sees them, she'll know her answer, and I'm not even ready to give an answer on this topic yet.

Am I? No. It's ridiculous. I can't be in love with him. Especially when the pattern would follow my mother's...I tell him I love him and he leaves.

No, Des. That's not what this is.

"For a woman who pushed me to sleep with Grant, why are you shying away from him?"

"I always shy away," I lie.

"That's such a load of crap and you know it."

"It's me. Do you know anyone who I've kept around longer than a few weeks? It's been a few weeks...so it's only inevitable what's going to happen next."

"Next? If I were you, I'd kick me and Taylor out and go in there and thank that man properly for installing a security system. Mm-mmm-mmm," she murmurs as she leans back in her chair so she can catch a glimpse of him. "Just his name—Reznor—it oozes sex and that bad-boy appeal and basically everything you love in a man...so the fact that you're hitting that hottie only a few times and then backing away slowly says you like him more than you're letting on."

And this is the problem with having a friend who knows you so well. She sees through all of your bullshit lies. *Even the ones you're telling yourself.*

"He's here for a short time."

"Exactly. Just how you like them—here and then gone—so tell me why you're not taking advantage of him?"

Because he's too close.

The thought repeats in my head later when the house is quiet and everyone has left. I walk back and forth in front of the infrared sensors Reznor installed just to watch them turn from green to red and back to distract me from thinking about my conversation with Emerson.

I'm not in love with Reznor.

She definitely has pregnancy brain if she's thinking that.

I can't be.

And yet one particular part of the conversation keeps replaying in my mind.

"So Grant says he's been trying to convince you to stay here in Sunnyville, Reznor."

Reznor stopped mid-motion as he released the chuck on his electric drill and nodded. "He has indeed."

"We're not exactly a small town anymore. I know we're not San Francisco, but we've grown a lot in the past few years. Now we have a lot more crazy," she says and laughs. "Grant thinks having an experienced SWAT commander is a good thing. Besides, it's safer here...and we have lots of wine."

I'm here, I thought.

"It won't be easy going back, that's for sure," he said as he looked at me, those brown eyes of his giving nothing away before looking back at Emerson. "But yeah, I'll be going back. My guys need me."

The pang of pain from his words hits me just as hard now as it did when he spoke them.

Maybe even harder. Because I hear other words about when he is leaving. *It could be sooner unless I find something here that piques my interest enough to want to stay.* And clearly, I haven't piqued his interest.

Em was wrong.

Admitting that hurts just as deeply.

I glance out the window toward his place, where the soft glow of the light reflects against his closed curtains.

Want to know the best way not to have your heart broken, Desi?

Keep your guard up, heart closed, mind clear. In other words, don't let yourself fall in love to begin with.

Chapter Twenty-Two

Reznor

"Coming," I yell in response to the knock on the door. I set down the book I was reading and head to answer it.

I'm surprised when I open it and see Desi standing there, bright orange sundress on, and a smile on her lips. "Hi there."

Jesus, that voice, that smile, does shit to my insides.

"Hi." It takes me a second to see the plate of cookies she's holding out to me. "You made me chocolate-chip cookies?" My stomach rumbles at the thought.

"I wanted to say thank you for the alarm system."

"No biggie," I say as I take the plate from her, pull the Saran Wrap off, and take a huge bite of one as I wave her in. "Oh my God." The cookie is incredible. I close my eyes and enjoy it. When I open them back up, Desi is watching me, and I don't give a flying fuck if it looks like I just came. I can't remember the last time someone baked for me who didn't share the same gene pool as me.

Our eyes meet, hold, and she shakes her head as if she's trying to remember why she came here.

"You didn't need to do that. The alarm. I mean...It was incredibly thoughtful of you."

She's nervous. Good. I like when she's flustered.

"I just wanted to make you feel a little bit more comfortable in your own house." I set the cookies down and don't say the obvious. *And because I'm going to worry about you when I'm gone and not living within shouting distance of you.*

"It has made me feel that way. Thank you...again."

We stare at each other, both measuring what exactly to say. Fuck it. I'll go there.

"I stopped by the other day."

"When?" she asks but I can see the shift in her eyes. I can tell she's nervous.

"Sunday. Monday. Earlier."

"Oh."

It's all she says—all she needs to say—for me to know my hunch was right. She was home, she heard me knocking on the door...but she decided she should shut me out.

Let me the fuck in, Desi. Ask me the million questions swimming in your eyes.

But she won't.

"Do you want to stay for dinner?"

She takes a deep breath, and I can see her fighting the need to leave. The need to avoid "more"—whatever the fuck way she defines more in that gorgeous brain of hers.

"I'd love to."

Thank fuck.

I looked her in the eyes and told her I'd be leaving soon and she showed no reaction. Yet, I still want her, and I'll take whatever I can get.

Clearly, I'm an idiot.

Chapter Twenty-Three

Desi

"Hey Des. Got a minute?"

"Hi, handsome," I say, recognizing Grant's voice as if it were my own brother's. "How are my babies doing?"

"Driving me crazy," he says through a laugh, but I can hear the absolute adoration in his tone and the smile on his lips.

"Isn't that the job of all women?" I shut the baby gate so the four pooches I'm dog-sitting are confined in their special room, and I can pick up the grooming area.

"Seems like it." He clears his throat. "I have some good news for you."

"Yeah?"

"They caught him."

I freeze mid-step and then stand there as those three words sink in. "They did?"

"Another house in Melville. Same scenario, except this time the husband happened to be sleeping on the couch and the perp didn't know it. Woman screamed, husband came...he may have roughed the fucker up to keep him until the police showed up, but...that's what he deserved."

"How do you know it's the same guy?" I ask, staring at the yard beyond and wondering how many nights since my incident I've stood here and wondered if someone was out there staring back at me, waiting until I go to bed to stand over me again.

"Because he confessed. I guess he had a box of shit, something he took from each house."

"Ugh." The thought that he had something of mine is enough to make my stomach churn. "Please tell me he didn't have a pair of my panties to sniff or something."

"Not yours, no. But he did have others. He had a Doggy Style business card and he had the date of his *visit* written on the back of it," he explains as chills creep over my skin at the thought of him touching anything of mine. "And I know what you're thinking, but no, you didn't know him. You did nothing to reject him or spur interest...it was just a random thing—which I don't know if that's creepier or not, but it's over."

"Thank you, Grant."

"I didn't do anything, but you're welcome."

I sag against the counter, and for what feels like the first time in months, I breathe a sigh of relief.

But when I hang up the phone, I know that's not true.

I breathed a huge sigh of relief the night Reznor took me to the haunted house and showed me that it was okay to be scared. That I didn't always have to be the strong one.

Without thinking, I drop the phone, run out the front door, and over to Reznor's.

For the first time, I don't have to think about what it is I want. I don't have to remind myself of the pact I made with myself to simply enjoy what little time I have left with him before he leaves. I don't have to tell my feelings to shut the hell down.

But when I knock on the front door—over and over—I realize that no one is home.

Reznor's not home.

And with each passing second, that excitement I felt moments before slowly comes crashing down around me. This is how it's going to be sooner rather than later.

Because this isn't Reznor's home.

He'll be gone.

He's not here now.

He'll be gone permanently very soon.

And I'll be here.

Alone.

Again.

Shit.

Chapter Twenty-Four

Desi

"Great work today, ladies," Reznor says as he smiles.

Yeah, my insides melt at the sight of it.

Just like they have for the past hour every time he touched me or addressed me. Of course, our interaction was purely professional because there was an audience, when all I wanted to do was sink into him and hold on for dear life.

But I didn't.

It was a rude but much-needed awakening when I knocked on his door and he wasn't home.

So I kept my distance. I didn't give him the flirty eyes or the little squeeze of his hand like I have in the past.

From the concerned look in his eyes I know he noticed. But was it concern or was it hurt that flickered there?

I'm not sure and I'm too busy protecting my heart to ask.

The same way I was when he came knocking on the door the other day to tell me how he relieved he was that they'd caught my intruder. I pretended to be on the phone with a supplier and that I couldn't talk with him.

Cowardly? Yes.

A necessity to save my heart from the impeding heartbreak? Definitely.

"Can I have one minute more of your time, ladies?" Bear asks just as we begin to walk off the mat. I nod eagerly, because that means one more minute to compose myself before I have to face Reznor.

The funny thing is that for the first time, I didn't come here today out of fear. I came here because I wanted to. Because I wanted to see Reznor.

I came because for the first time in forever, I felt okay.

"Who here has enjoyed working with Rez?" Bear asks.

Hoots and hollers echo off the gym as women applaud and praise him. Reznor looks at Bear—his cheeks slightly flushed in embarrassment—and then shakes his head before looking over and locking his eyes on mine.

The look in his eyes and the pulse of the muscle in his jaw—I already know what Bear is going to say before he speaks.

"Next week will be our last class with Reznor unless you can convince him to stay." The women around me groan while I stand stoically.

And my heart implodes.

No. I don't know if I say the word or if I scream it, but it's on repeat in my head, even though that simple word does nothing to truly express how I feel inside. How it feels to have your insides drop to your toes while your body has to keep operating.

"He's been called back to SFPD...some shit about them needing him. Don't they know we need him?" He laughs.

Don't they know I need him?

Bear drones on, but it's Reznor's eyes I can't look away from. It's his broad shoulders and proud posture I want to hold on to. It's those strong arms I want to wrap around me.

But they won't.

I knew this was coming...and yet I didn't expect to find out like this.

I didn't expect to hear it secondhand from Bear and not from Reznor himself...and that stings. I feel...angry suddenly, and although I don't really have the right to direct it at Reznor, that's where it is. It's fueled by hurt and heartache and disbelief, and I...*I need to get out of here.*

But he keeps staring at me.

I can't stand here anymore.

I'm mad at myself for doing the one thing I swore I couldn't—fall for Reznor. And now I have and he's leaving regardless, so who looks like the idiot now?

It's all my fault. I've got to get out of here.

"Excuse me," I murmur to the lady beside me as I step back and off the mat as Bear continues.

I quickly grab my things and jog out of the gym, trying not to call attention to myself. My feet move to staunch my anger but my head and heart keep fueling it.

"Desi. Wait up."

And his voice...his voice fuels it too.

"Leave me alone, Reznor." Hurt, pain, heartache—all three spin an eddy of discord through me that I don't want to feel.

"Des?" More footsteps on the pavement beside me.

I walk right past my car and out of the parking lot—needing space, needing privacy, needing to get away from him as my eyes burn and my chest aches.

Once I clear the corner and we're out of eyeshot of most of the class, he grabs my arm. Within an instant, I've spun around, locked his arm with mine, and have my knee coming up to his groin in a move we've practiced many times in class.

"Whoa there," he says, counteracting me and pinning my arms to protect himself. The laugh he emits only serves to irritate me further. "Well, at least I know I did my job and you can protect yourself."

Yep. You did your job. That's all it was.

"It's not funny," I say through gritted teeth, as I yank my arms free of his and stride ahead of him.

"I know it's not." He jogs beside me, but I refuse to look his way.

"You couldn't tell me yourself? You had to let me find out from Bear—in front of the whole class—that you were leaving?"

God. As much as I didn't want more, right now I do, and hell if it doesn't sting being the one on the other end of the situation I've always controlled.

"I was going to tell you, Des."

"When?"

"After class."

"Wow. Thanks. I'm surprised you weren't going to sleep with me so you could guarantee one more quick romp before you told me."

"That's not how it is, and you know it."

"Then how is it?"

This time when he grabs my arm, I don't fight him. I'm out of breath and hurt, and I stop in the middle of the sidewalk with his hand on my arm and my eyes asking questions my mouth isn't ready to put a voice to.

"I had a finite amount of time here. We both knew that," he says. *Yeah, but maybe I didn't want to believe it.* "Besides, it's hard to talk to someone—tell someone something—when they're already shutting down on you."

"I was not," I shout.

"Really? You're ready to die by that sword, Des, because it seems to me you've made it a habit to be busy any time I've come around in the past few days. Or maybe you've already moved on to the next person, huh?"

"Don't be an ass."

"Don't push me away."

We stand and stare at each other in the waning light of the sunset, and I'm all out of things to say to him. All I can focus on is this stabbing ache in my heart. It's the reason I've never gotten close to someone before, and it's much easier to focus on that than how damn handsome he is and the pleading look in his eyes.

"We have a week left. We can make the most of it and—"

"Don't bother, Reznor," I say while my heart screams *yes, please.*

"Don't be like that. We can—"

"We can what? Have sex a few more times for old times' sake? Wow. Thanks for thinking of me. That would only result in me..." *In me falling for you more than I already have when I know I can't have you.*

"I care about you. I don't want to hurt you."

Hurt me? At least he's made things crystal clear. It would have no impact on his heart if he spent more time with me before he left. I would be his Sunnyville booty call.

No. Fuck you.

"Then don't. Do me a favor and let this be it. Save me from...just let this be it." My voice breaks along with every other part of me when I step up and press a soft kiss to his cheek. "Goodbye, Reznor."

And when I walk down the sidewalk, this time he doesn't follow.

Chapter Twenty-Five

Desi

"Grant says Reznor's been trying to get hold of you."

"Stay out of it, Emerson." I sigh into the phone as I pound my fist on the table when my computer doesn't do what I need it to do.

Nothing like attempting to design your own website when you're computer illiterate so you can keep yourself busy.

"He lives like forty feet or whatever it is away from you...what did you do? Close all your blinds so you can't see his house?"

I glance over to my blinds that are just that and pinch the bridge of my nose. "I asked you to stay out of this, Em. Please. I need to do this my way."

She must hear the desperation in my voice because the line falls silent. "It doesn't have to be this way. It—"

"Yes, it does."

I hang up the phone, not wanting to hear it anymore.

This is what I need to do.

This is how I have to do it.

This is how I protect myself from getting hurt further.

I have to shut him out.

Just like all the times he's come knocking on the door this week. Like how on Sunday when I came home from a girls' night out, I didn't say thank you after noticing he'd taken my delivery of bagged dog food, carried it to the back of the house, and put it in storage bins like he'd watched me do before. Or how on Monday, my lawn was mowed and the hedges had been trimmed. Or better yet, on Tuesday, how he pulled my trash cans out to the curb for me so I wouldn't have to struggle with them since they were so full and heavy.

All the things I don't need to remember him doing. The thoughtful things I wish he wouldn't do so I'm not reminded of what a great guy he is...and how much I'm going to miss him.

Chapter Twenty-Six

Desi

"Pussy, I'm really over you and your nails clawing me," I say to the drowned-looking cat whose fur is flattened by water, making her body look a third of what it does when it's dry.

And there's something about the moment, about the damn cat, that brings up the memory of the first time I learned Reznor was my neighbor. This cat was the catalyst bringing us together.

The thought makes my heart lurch. Panic consumes me as I take the wet cat and put her in a crate, and without thinking of anything else, run out the back door as fast as I can. The gate to the side yard sticks, and I struggle with it momentarily before I shove it open.

My fist pounds on Reznor's door.

Pure panic. It's the kind that tells you that if you don't act now, you're going to miss out.

Knock-knock.

The kind that says, I'm sorry, but I really do need just one more night with you. Not just for the sex. More because I need to tell you how I feel about you.

My hand stutters at the revelation. Because I do have feelings for him.

Tons of them.

Holy shit.

Knock-knock-knock.

I use more force this time. More urgency.

I slide to the side of the door and cup my hands against the window and peer inside.

He's gone.

The furniture is still there, as it was rented, but every little piece of him that made it his is gone.

Just like that.

I lower myself to the step as the tears well and then slip down my cheeks.

You said don't bother, Des.

This is what it feels like when your heart is breaking.

This one is on you.

Chapter Twenty-Seven

Desi

"Thank you for inviting me...again"— I chuckle into the phone – "but I've got a full house today, and I'm already behind schedule."

"It's been two months, Des."

"Two months since what?" I ask, even though I know damn well what she's saying. It's been two months since Reznor left, and I'm still licking my wounds and pretending I'm not nursing a broken heart.

"Just call him already, will you?"

"And say what? Drop your life and come back here, because I don't know how to commit to anyone and I can't make you any promises, but I want to try? That maybe I can figure out how to change my ways, and we can live in our own kind of happily ever after where we don't get married but we are together?"

"That's a good start."

But it's not Emerson who says those words. It's the deep tenor voice from my back door.

I gasp as I turn to see Reznor standing there. He's wearing his police uniform that fits his personality and doesn't fit it, all at the same time.

"Reznor?"

"What?" Emerson asks the same time Reznor says, "Ooops, I didn't mean to scare you. I forgot."

Knock-knock. Knock-knock-knock.

"Em? I have to go." I don't even know if I end the call or not. I drop my cell on the counter with a clatter as my feet move involuntarily toward the screen.

Reznor has a ghost of a smile on his lips and caution edged with hope in his eyes.

"We don't want any," I say without any conviction as I stop a few feet from him.

"Yeah well, we already know how far that got us, so this time, it's my turn to lead." That rasp of voice—*with hints of gravel and grit to it*—sounds like music to my ears.

"What are you doing here?" My heart pounds a strident staccato and my head begs him to answer that he's here for me.

"I had a meeting with Sunnyville PD."

"Oh."

"And because I think we went about this all wrong."

There's a lump in my throat I can't seem to swallow. He leans his shoulder against the doorjamb and stares at me with those mesmerizing eyes of his. I've imagined this moment in my head many times over the past few weeks and yet nothing could have prepared me for what it feels like to see him again.

"Why's that?" I ask.

"Because we have. I told you once that my life was all about control. Who has it. Who wants it. How to transfer it from one person to another with the least amount of damage to everyone involved...and I think I applied that to what was between you and me. I was wrong." He takes a step toward me, and my breath hitches when he reaches out and cups the side of my cheek.

"Reznor?" My voice breaks simply saying his name.

"I left here thinking that so long as we experienced the least amount of damage, that I did the right thing...but you know what? Screw the right thing, Desi. Screw societal standards that say a happy couple has to be a married one. Screw the fact that I was too afraid to say I'd fallen for you because I thought you'd run for the hills...and I knew I was in no state of mind to chase you." He steps into me and places his hands on my hips and stares at me with eyes full of emotion. "I've fallen for you, Desi Whitman, and I'm back here to chase you."

"What do you mean back here?"

"I just had an interview with Chief Ramos."

"Wait...you're—"

"I've been offered a job with SPD."

"I don't...how did—what? You love your job with SWAT."

"Yeah, but it's time I have a job where I can have someone I go home to every night without worrying about what might happen. Sure, the police department is still dangerous, but it's not SWAT."

"You're serious," I say almost as if to make sure I'm hearing him right.

"As a heart attack." Reznor leans in and kisses me. It's soft and tender and resonates through every part of me. "Tell me you're okay with me wanting to come back here. Tell me you want this," he murmurs against my lips.

"I'll do even better than that." I lean forward and kiss him back. "I've fallen head over heels for you too, Reznor Mayne. It took you leaving for me to realize it, but there hasn't been a day since that I haven't thought about it. About you. *About us.*"

"Then why didn't you call me?" He chuckles, and the sound feels so good as it vibrates against my chest.

"I warned you. I'm stubborn."

He leans back and looks at me, his smile reaching his eyes. "I think I can handle you."

"You *think* you can?"

"Sweetheart, *I know* I can." His lips slant over mine again and something inside my heart and body clicks back into place.

For the first time they are on the same page.

I want this. *I want us.*

Our story will not be the typical happily ever after, because that's for the movies. We will fight. We will fuck. We will laugh and give each other hell. And then we'll have a helluva time making up. But I doubt our hunger will ever abate, because this easy-going, hard-fighting, good-looking man wants me.

He wants us.

I look at him, and I *just know*. This is going to work. Because Reznor has made me see that love isn't about maintaining control. It's about ceding control because you know that love offers strength. It's about one being strong when the other needs to be weak. It's about balancing the other out.

It's about making it work on our terms.

For us.

* * * *

Also from 1001 Dark Nights and K. Bromberg, discover Sweet Rivalry.

Sign up for the 1001 Dark Nights Newsletter
and be entered to win a Tiffany Key necklace.

There's a contest every month!

Go to www.1001DarkNights.com to subscribe.

As a bonus, all subscribers will receive a free copy of
Discovery Bundle Three
Featuring stories by
Sidney Bristol, Darcy Burke, T. Gephart
Stacey Kennedy, Adriana Locke
JB Salsbury, and Erika Wilde

Discover 1001 Dark Nights Collection Five

Go to www.100DarkNights.com for more information

BLAZE ERUPTING by Rebecca Zanetti
Scorpius Syndrome/A Brigade Novella

ROUGH RIDE by Kristen Ashley
A Chaos Novella

HAWKYN by Larissa Ione
A Demonica Underworld Novella

RIDE DIRTY by Laura Kaye
A Raven Riders Novella

ROME'S CHANCE by Joanna Wylde
A Reapers MC Novella

THE MARRIAGE ARRANGEMENT by Jennifer Probst
A Marriage to a Billionaire Novella

SURRENDER by Elisabeth Naughton
A House of Sin Novella

INKED NIGHT by Carrie Ann Ryan
A Montgomery Ink Novella

ENVY by Rachel Van Dyken
An Eagle Elite Novella

PROTECTED by Lexi Blake
A Masters and Mercenaries Novella

THE PRINCE by Jennifer L. Armentrout
A Wicked Novella

PLEASE ME by J. Kenner
A Stark Ever After Novella

WOUND TIGHT by Lorelei James
A Rough Riders/Blacktop Cowboys Novella®

STRONG by Kylie Scott
A Stage Dive Novella

DRAGON NIGHT by Donna Grant
A Dark Kings Novella

TEMPTING BROOKE by Kristen Proby
A Big Sky Novella

HAUNTED BE THE HOLIDAYS by Heather Graham
A Krewe of Hunters Novella

CONTROL by K. Bromberg
An Everyday Heroes Novella

HUNKY HEARTBREAKER by Kendall Ryan
A Whiskey Kisses Novella

THE DARKEST CAPTIVE by Gena Showalter
A Lords of the Underworld Novella

Discover 1001 Dark Nights Collection One

Go to www.100DarkNights.com for more information

FOREVER WICKED by Shayla Black
CRIMSON TWILIGHT by Heather Graham
CAPTURED IN SURRENDER by Liliana Hart
SILENT BITE: A SCANGUARDS WEDDING by Tina Folsom
DUNGEON GAMES by Lexi Blake
AZAGOTH by Larissa Ione
NEED YOU NOW by Lisa Renee Jones
SHOW ME, BABY by Cherise Sinclair
ROPED IN by Lorelei James
TEMPTED BY MIDNIGHT by Lara Adrian
THE FLAME by Christopher Rice
CARESS OF DARKNESS by Julie Kenner

Also from 1001 Dark Nights

TAME ME by J. Kenner

Discover 1001 Dark Nights Collection Two

Go to www.100DarkNights.com for more information

WICKED WOLF by Carrie Ann Ryan
WHEN IRISH EYES ARE HAUNTING by Heather Graham
EASY WITH YOU by Kristen Proby
MASTER OF FREEDOM by Cherise Sinclair
CARESS OF PLEASURE by Julie Kenner
ADORED by Lexi Blake
HADES by Larissa Ione
RAVAGED by Elisabeth Naughton
DREAM OF YOU by Jennifer L. Armentrout
STRIPPED DOWN by Lorelei James
RAGE/KILLIAN by Alexandra Ivy/Laura Wright
DRAGON KING by Donna Grant
PURE WICKED by Shayla Black
HARD AS STEEL by Laura Kaye
STROKE OF MIDNIGHT by Lara Adrian
ALL HALLOWS EVE by Heather Graham
KISS THE FLAME by Christopher Rice
DARING HER LOVE by Melissa Foster
TEASED by Rebecca Zanetti
THE PROMISE OF SURRENDER by Liliana Hart

Also from 1001 Dark Nights

THE SURRENDER GATE By Christopher Rice
SERVICING THE TARGET By Cherise Sinclair

Discover 1001 Dark Nights Collection Three

Go to www.100DarkNights.com for more information

HIDDEN INK by Carrie Ann Ryan
BLOOD ON THE BAYOU by Heather Graham
SEARCHING FOR MINE by Jennifer Probst
DANCE OF DESIRE by Christopher Rice
ROUGH RHYTHM by Tessa Bailey
DEVOTED by Lexi Blake
Z by Larissa Ione
FALLING UNDER YOU by Laurelin Paige
EASY FOR KEEPS by Kristen Proby
UNCHAINED by Elisabeth Naughton
HARD TO SERVE by Laura Kaye
DRAGON FEVER by Donna Grant
KAYDEN/SIMON by Alexandra Ivy/Laura Wright
STRUNG UP by Lorelei James
MIDNIGHT UNTAMED by Lara Adrian
TRICKED by Rebecca Zanetti
DIRTY WICKED by Shayla Black
THE ONLY ONE by Lauren Blakely
SWEET SURRENDER by Liliana Hart

Discover 1001 Dark Nights Collection Four

Go to www.100DarkNights.com for more information

ROCK CHICK REAWAKENING by Kristen Ashley
ADORING INK by Carrie Ann Ryan
SWEET RIVALRY by K. Bromberg
SHADE'S LADY by Joanna Wylde
RAZR by Larissa Ione
ARRANGED by Lexi Blake
TANGLED by Rebecca Zanetti
HOLD ME by J. Kenner
SOMEHOW, SOME WAY by Jennifer Probst
TOO CLOSE TO CALL by Tessa Bailey
HUNTED by Elisabeth Naughton
EYES ON YOU by Laura Kaye
BLADE by Alexandra Ivy/Laura Wright
DRAGON BURN by Donna Grant
TRIPPED OUT by Lorelei James
STUD FINDER by Lauren Blakely
MIDNIGHT UNLEASHED by Lara Adrian
HALLOW BE THE HAUNT by Heather Graham
DIRTY FILTHY FIX by Laurelin Paige
THE BED MATE by Kendall Ryan
PRINCE ROMAN by CD Reiss
NO RESERVATIONS by Kristen Proby
DAWN OF SURRENDER by Liliana Hart

Also from 1001 Dark Nights

Tempt Me by J. Kenner

About K. Bromberg

New York Times Bestselling author K. Bromberg writes contemporary romance novels that contain a mixture of sweet, emotional, a whole lot of sexy, and a little bit of real. She likes to write strong heroines and damaged heroes who we love to hate but can't help to love.

A mom of three, she plots her novels in between school runs and soccer practices, more often than not with her laptop in tow and her mind scattered in too many different directions.

Since publishing her first book on a whim in 2013, Kristy has sold over one and a half million copies of her books across eighteen different countries and has landed on the *New York Times*, *USA Today*, and *Wall Street Journal* Bestsellers lists over thirty times. Her Driven trilogy (Driven, Fueled, and Crashed) is currently being adapted for film by the streaming platform, Passionflix, with the first movie (Driven) out now.

With her imagination always in overdrive, she is currently scheming, plotting, and swooning over her latest hero. You can find out more about him or chat with Kristy on any of her social media accounts. The easiest way to stay up to date on new releases and upcoming novels is to sign up for her newsletter (http://bit.ly/254MWtI) or text KBromberg to 77948 to receive text alerts when a new book releases.

Discover More K. Bromberg

SWEET RIVALRY

By K. Bromberg

Ryder Rodgers had a plan.

He was going to stride into the conference room, do the required song and dance over the next five days, and win the biggest contract of his career. But when he walked in and heard the voice of one of his competitors, all his plans were shot to hell.

Harper Denton. She was always on top. *In college.* First in their class. Always using every advantage to edge him out to win the coveted positions. The only one who could beat him. His academic rival. *More like a constant thorn in his side.* And his ego's.

When he heard her voice, he was brought back to years before. To the bitter taste of being second best. But the woman who meets his gaze is nothing like the drab wallflower he used to know. *Hell no.* She was all woman now: curves, confidence, and staggering sex appeal. And no doubt, *still brilliant.*

The fact that she's gorgeous *and* bright won't distract him. This time, Ryder's determined to be the one on top. *But not if Harper can help it.*

On behalf of 1001 Dark Nights,

Liz Berry and M.J. Rose would like to thank ~

Steve Berry
Doug Scofield
Kim Guidroz
Jillian Stein
InkSlinger PR
Dan Slater
Asha Hossain
Chris Graham
Fedora Chen
Kasi Alexander
Jessica Johns
Dylan Stockton
Richard Blake
and Simon Lipskar

Made in the USA
Coppell, TX
04 February 2021